THE LIGHTHOUSE

A Supernatural
Romance Thriller

KAREN POWER

ISBN: 978-0-6450435-5-6 (paperback)
ISBN 978-0-6450435-6-3 (e-book)
ISBN: 978-0-6450435-2-5 (audiobook)

Book cover photo: Prescot Horn from Unsplash

A catalogue record for this book is available from the National Library of Australia

DEDICATION

This book is dedicated to my very dear Mother, who prays for me always, and my very close friends who are always so supportive of my creative endeavors.

Karen Power xoxo

One

Dying rays of sunset stream through black billowing storm clouds on the horizon as dusk descends across the skyline. A trendy little coupé nips along a winding, windswept road as darkness falls. Kian McGregor, early-thirties, very long black hair, attractive but with a tear-streaked face, drives with mounting recklessness. The back seat is crammed with suitcases. Kian roars around a corner. A flash appears, a dark shape swiftly glides across the road in front of Kian's car. Kian suddenly slams on the brakes. The car swerves off the road and screeches to a gravel spitting halt in front of a giant, monolithic rock formation. The headlights shine directly onto a sign, "WELCOME TO WOLF ROCK POINT." The driver's door flings open, and Kian almost tumbles out. She quickly regains her composure, unsure of what she had seen, then Kian scours the roadside to see if she hit anything.

There is nothing in sight. The chilling wind sounds send chills down Kian's spine. Then in the dark, she investigates the side of the car further. Kian now notices the front tire is flat. She opens the car trunk, rummages around, looking for the jack. Angst to find there is not one available. Kian mutters to herself as she finds a tool to fix the tire. She is startled by an owl flying directly overhead in the night.

Now highly stressed, Kian whips out her cell phone, flips it open, and jabs in a number. A message appears, "NO SERVICE AVAILABLE." Frustrated and in despair, Kian slams the trunk shut and looks around at the dark, gloomy unknown surroundings she has suddenly found herself in. A thunderous crack of lightning explodes from the heavens, and the fast-approaching storm reveals ahead an old Lighthouse atop the nearby cliff. The gigantic old tree next to the Lighthouse sways ferociously in the stormy wind.

For a moment, Kian regards the creepy old Lighthouse and its towering spooky presence, silhouetted against the flashes of lightning. With the rain now teaming down and nowhere to go, she makes her way up a winding muddy path toward the Lighthouse, seeking shelter from the cold, wet rain.

Kian approaches the deserted front porch of the Lighthouse. Squinting to see in the dark, she vaguely makes out a sizeable handwritten sign mounted on a tall single post prominently positioned right outside the Lighthouse front steps. The sign flapping in the ferocious wind reveals the words. "FOR RENT." Another sign hangs on the front door displaying the same message.

Kian knocks on the antiquated old wooden door using the brass knocker. Even in the storm, it sounds loud and echoes. Kian was tense, aware of her nervous breathing. In the dark of the night, she awaits a response to her knocking. Shivering, she knocks again, and there is no response. Kian steps back off the porch and looks up above toward the elevated upper higher levels of the Lighthouse, which eerily stands majestic against the backdrop of the haunting sky.

The rain beats down heavily. In the dismal light, Kian checks her cell phone.

Again she sees the message, "NO SERVICE AVAILABLE." Kian glances back down the road toward her parked car, then worriedly scours the bleak deserted surroundings. She sighs, frustrated. A powerful gust of wind rises. On her left side, a dark transparent shape swiftly passes by her.

Kian shivers in the dark and slowly turns her head back toward the door. The large old wooden door of the Lighthouse slowly slightly creaks open. Kian turns to face the door, shudders, and stands there fearful. Hesitant though curious, she stares at the partially opened door, not sure what to make of it.

Kian approaches the porch again, her heart beating rapidly. Once more, still feeling apprehensive, Kian stops and tries to peer inside through the slightly ajar door. She calls, "Hello, is anyone there?" Her voice echoes to the inside then silence reigns from the dark shadowy opening.

Kian heaves the heavy wooden door all the way open and takes a small step inside.

By mistake, her arm catches her long, now very wet hair, suddenly pulling her head backward. Scaring herself and on edge, Kian leans slightly further inside the dark abyss of the old building. She calls again, "Hello. Anybody here?" Still nothing. Kian cautiously enters the shroud of darkness as she anticipates a response. The sudden bolts of lightning illuminate bare wooden floorboards, revealing the shapes of furniture covered with old dusty canvas sheets.

On guard, Kian enters the Lighthouse, moving ever so slowly. She finds a fire stoker rod leaning against the wall, which she grabs. She tightly holds it up in the air for safety. Kian calls again loudly. "Hello?"

All that can be heard is the thunder and scary howling winds outside.

The windows rattle ferociously as the rain beats down on them. Kian jabs the cell phone keypad again. This time the screen lights up. Temporarily relieved, Kian expels a deep breath of relief then holds the phone up, using its light to illuminate her way as she continues to explore her surroundings, moving further forward into the old musty Lighthouse.

Kian creeps slowly around the big dusty table and chairs in the rustic kitchen. Unable to see clearly in the darkness, she accidentally stubs her toe on an old cast iron rod on the floor. She grabs her toe to ease the pain.

Whimpering, she searches for somewhere to sit to nurture her foot to decrease the pain. But she stumbles across an old wooden steep spiral stairway, stops, and curiously looks up. She shines her phone torch upwards to see better with the small light. It looks like the rickety old staircase spirals upwards for two or more floors.

Kian hobbles for a moment, then cautiously makes her way up the winding staircase and onto the first-floor landing. She discovers a door, pushes and pulls the doorknob struggling to open it. It seems jammed locked. Once again, exerting full strength, she tries hard. The door suddenly flies open, and she loses balance, falling, hitting the floor hard from the impact. Dust rises into the air around her, taking her breath away.

Kian's coughing echoes across the dismal gloomy room.

She stares into the dark of the creepy room, vulnerable and sad, tears beginning to well up and roll down her sad, melancholy face. The dark shadow observes, hovering in solemn silence in the morbid corner of the room, undetected lingering close to the heavy musty tapestry curtains. Once again uses her phone as a torch and scans the large old room. She sees a large old double bed and wardrobes covered with dusty canvas sheets. Kian steps further into the middle of the room. She moves to the bed and pulls the canvas off to reveal an old antique gold iron double bed. Kian sits down and tests the mattress. Then she gets up, goes to the window, looks outside. There is nothing but rain, lightning, thunder, and the loud howling wind.

Below in the distance, strong bolts of lightning light up her car parked off the side of the road. Although bogged, she sees it is well off the road, so not a threat to any other drivers. Her sad beautiful face looks even more tired. She sits down on the bed again, wondering what to do next. The raindrops pelt down firmly against the rattling window. Exhausted, she falls back onto the bed and temporarily falls asleep. The dark silhouette hovers around the outer walls of the spooky room, observing the vulnerable sleeping Kian. The floorboards creak eerily. A sudden bolt of lightning rushes through the windowpane for a second, lighting up the silhouette's most blue piercing frightened eyes staring at Kian.

Kian wakes and sits bolt upright. Startled and frightened by the lightning, Kian scans the blackness of the room to see if anyone else has entered the room. She is still alone and vulnerable in the shadows.

Impulsively Kian races out of the room and frantically

down the stairs leaving the front door ajar as she swiftly exits the Lighthouse. She runs fleetly in the wet rain back to her bogged car. The rain teaming down as she opens the side passenger seat of the vehicle and drags out the large suitcases. As quickly as possible, Kian grabs them and runs back to the Lighthouse, her thin frame almost toppling over, trying to carry the sheer weight of the bulging suitcases. She struggles through the slippery thick mud track, back up to the damp- ness of the Lighthouse. Once again, she enters the lonely dark abyss and slams the door shut behind her. She drags the suit- cases inside toward the staircase. She sits on the bottom of the stairs, trying to undo the suitcase zip. The door suddenly slowly creeks eerily open slightly, then instantly slams shut behind her.

The loud sound echoes throughout the Lighthouse. Kian is frightened: she shudders, stops for a moment as her eyes frantically scan the darkness of her immediate surroundings. Short of breath sitting on the bottom of the stairs, she is now emotionally exhausted. She cradles her knees tightly into her cold, shivering body and begins to cry until she runs out of tears. In the chilly dark corner of the room, the creepy silent silhouette hovers intensely regarding Kian.

Still shivering, Kian sadly opens one of the suitcases and rummages around in the dark, trying to find something warm to put on. She finds a towel and pats herself down with it to soak up the excess water dripping from her clothes, then wraps up her very long black wet hair.

She takes off her muddy shoes, placing them slightly away from her, then covers her body over with a couple of jumpers, grabs some of the clothes out, and lays them on the floor. She lowers her cold, shivering body down on them, and then she snuggles up to her suitcases using one as a pillow. She places the fire stoker within hands reach next to her for safety.

Too tired to question her actions. She discovers her small toy rabbit as she pulls out her small baby hand quilted blanket from the suitcase. Softly sobbing, she snuggles the toy rabbit into her chest, wrapping herself up in the hand-quilted baby blanket. Kian drifts off into a deep sleep. The dark penetrating eyes stare, watching on for hours as Kian drifts into the deeper rems.

The shadowy dark figure lurks around the other suitcase, only inches away from the sleeping Kian. The other scattered clothes on the floor lift high into the air. The bag opens up simultaneously, the clothes fly straight into the suitcase, the suitcase zipper zips up swiftly, and the case stands on its side. The case slides aggressively over to the front door as Kian's muddy shoes follow suit and slide across the dusty floor, then come to rest suddenly leaning up against the suitcase. The creaking door opens slightly to reveal the howling winds again outside. The door loudly slams shut. The sudden impact wakes Kian.

She was slightly energized after a deep sleep. Kian gets up, stretches her stiff waif-like body, then places the soft toy rabbit on the blanket on top of the suitcase, which lays right next to her.

Kian uses her phone torch to see and goes into the old kitchen. She rummages through the drawers and cupboards of the enormous old kitchen. She finds some candles, glass cups, and a portable gas lighter. Enthusiastically Kian lights the portable gas lighter, which sheds an ample warm glow lighting up her surroundings. She lights a candle and places it into a glass cup that she uses to stand the candle. She dashes back to the front foyer area and forages around in her suitcase, pulling out a bottle of red wine from the case. She pops the cork, and red wine pours into her glass cup. Kian removes the hand-made baby quilt from her suitcase, wraps herself in it, then relaxes in an old large leather armchair with her glass of red wine. Kian can see it is still wet and frighteningly windy outside through the large glass window.

Kian distracts herself and flicks through the phone book in her cell phone. And she stops at a name, "JASON." She regards the name for a moment, then presses "CALL." But the message "NO SERVICE AVAILABLE" appears again.

Kian flips the phone shut, and forlornly she stares toward the darkness of the ceiling. She takes a long slow breath. Deep in thought, she sips more red wine until the glass is empty. She closes her eyes and settles into the armchair, getting comfortable once again, drifting into a heavy slumber.

In black and white slow motion, Kian, dressed in a white hospital gown, her face gaunt, eyes dark, walks along a deserted corridor. She stops at a Nursery Viewing Room. She gazes through the window. The nursery is full of newborn babies, all sleeping peacefully. Then it starts to snow inside the nursery. Snowflakes flutter down onto the beautiful babies, covering the nursery in a blanket of white. Then a huge Klan-Clad Sword materializes and floats in the air just above the cribs. A baby begins whimpering, then moaning, as if in pain. Kian, standing and watching from the outside of the room, bangs urgently on the window, yelling something.

Kian's eyes suddenly fly open, awakened by fear. She bolts

upright from her dream. It's pitch black again in the Lighthouse. But we still hear a baby moaning. So does Kian. She shakes her head and listens into the dark of the night. Nervous, she fumbles around trying to find the matches, lights the candle. Kian gets to her feet and slowly follows the moaning out to see where it is coming from. Kian stops at the foot of the staircase and listens to the haunting whimpering which seems to be emanating from the upper level. Kian, apprehensive, climbs a few steps, then suddenly stops.

Emotional, she calls out in desperation, "Hello." The moaning stops. Silence reigns once again, except for the howling wind outside. Uneasy, Kian scours the candlelit surroundings. Her cell phone suddenly rings aloud, scaring her with its piercing ring. Kian jumps back, dropping the candle. She fumbles the phone from her pocket, flips it open. The caller, I.D. reads "JASON."

Kian hesitates, then jabs the answer button. Kian, unsettled, answers, "Hello, Hello." Kian remains silent while she listens to Jason speak on the other end. Jason pleads with Kian that he doesn't want to fight, they don't have to go down this road, and she doesn't have to leave. Kian listens on the phone and still doesn't respond. Over the telephone, Jason apologizes and tries to reason with Kian, telling her he is weak and is looking for someone to blame for his emotional state. Kian sharply responds by correcting him by stating, "you mean someone to hurt."

Kian holds the phone close to her ear, tearing up as Jason continues to beg her to come back to him. She takes a long silent beat, then musters up all her strength, then blurts out, "it's not going to happen." Jason grapples with Kian over the phone, yelling, "Why not?" Kian, devastated, stares apathetic into space, then in a timid, sad frail voice, she answers slowly, "I don't know."

Emotionally empty, her eyes searching the surroundings of the Lighthouse. Kian, assertive this time, speaks again into the phone to Jason, "Somewhere I can clear my mind ... maybe even try writing again."

Jason sternly responds negatively over the phone. "You want to go through that kind of rejection? Again?" Kian, silently angry, doesn't answer. Jason sighs exacerbated, over the phone, "Please, Kian, "You're not a writer. You're my wife."

Kian, furious at his words, reactive, ferociously snaps the phone shut. The dark shadow still silently hovers in the corner, staring on, unsure of what is playing out.

Kian, mad as hell, fiercely opens the front door and, with intense determination, steps out into the vigor of the wind. Like a warrior wrenching off the "FOR RENT" sign at the front step of the Lighthouse, she throws it hard onto the wet boggy ground. The rain lashes down on it, and puddles of mud splash onto it.

Kian goes back into the darkness of the Lighthouse and throws herself into the large old armchair. She punches the armrest hard.

Tearing up with tears of frustration and anguish, she sobs. Sinking further into the armchair, she stares up to the ceiling in a trance-like state. Her eyes close once more, eventually drifting back into a deep sleep.

Two

The beginning of sunrise dawns, throwing soft rays of light through the misty thick rain clouds exposing the monolithic rock formation surrounding the Lighthouse, above the ocean, with the waves crashing into its rock-solid foundation below. Strong winds thrash at the enormous 100-year-old tree standing next to the Lighthouse. Its boughs bend, and branches whip one of the historic headstones in the small graveyard. The strong branch returns to balance at each eerie rise and fall of the whistling winds. The sun's subtle early morning rays shed more light on the surrounding landscape and the lonely solitude of the small cemetery.

Back down on the main road, Kian waves goodbye as a Road Assistance Vehicle drives off after replacing her car's flat tire. She jumps back into the little coupé. She drives up the very muddy lubricious road back to the Lighthouse with incredible difficulty. The dark shadow hovers just inside the window, staring intensely, observing everything.

Kian, loud and with great effort, hauls in the last of her suitcases and dumps it alongside the rest of her belongings. She pulls back the heavy curtains. Daylight streams in. She begins to pull off the canvas coverings and drags them off the furniture, throwing up a cloud of dust and revealing new Art Deco furnishings. The dark shadowy figure slowly and quietly closes the curtains in the kitchen, dimming the light. Kian enters the room. She looks around in the half-dark room, slightly bewildered, then goes to the kitchen window and opens the curtain and the window itself to let in the fresh sea air. She takes a deep breath and peers out the window over the turbulent ocean.

The dark shadow hovers in the corner, overwhelmed by the sudden rush of sea air. Unseen by Kian, it silently exits the kitchen. Kian hauls her suitcase up the stairs, the sound echoing loudly, disturbing the silence of the Lighthouse.

Kian enters the bedroom on the first floor and opens the curtains in the half-lit room. She lifts the canvas coverings off the wardrobes then throws her suitcase onto the bed.

Kian climbs the next flight of stairs, encountering another door. Her frail arm fought to open it. Finally, it scrapes open slightly. It is very dark inside. Kian cannot see in and starts to enter. The wind suddenly rises, and the door slams hard, locking her out. Behind the locked door, we see the dark shadow which appears to be sitting on a sizable old rocking tapestry armchair. The dark shadow's fervent blue eyes show an unknown fear, intensely staring at the now locked door.

Kian curious climbs the stairs further right to the top then enters the old Lantern Room, now converted into a study with a 360-degree view of the surroundings through large glass windows. Kian unlocks the French doors and steps out onto the windy balcony. Beginning to relax, she closes her eyes, takes a deep breath enjoying the fresh sea air, then, for a long moment, admires the beauty of the panoramic view over the ocean outstretched before her.

Later, back downstairs in the bedroom on the first floor, Kian sifts through all her gear, locates a portable CD player, slips in a disc, presses play. Classical Music fills the Lighthouse as Kian slips into a pair of overalls. She opens one of her suitcases. It's full of cleaning products. She pulls out a couple of thick rubber gloves, new cleaning cloths still in the packets, garbage bag liners, and a selection of cleaning products. Kian discovers the laundry and rummages through the cupboards, pulls out an old broom, bucket and mop.

Back in the kitchen, Kian boils water and carefully pours it into the mop bucket. She empties a whole bottle of disinfectant into the bucket and stands the mop and broom in it. With renewed enthusiasm, Kian sweeps and mops the dark slate hallway floor.

On the first floor again. Kian sprays window cleaner on the dresser mirror then aggressively wipes it clean. She stands back to admire how spic and span the mirror looks.

Kian mops the slate hall floor again. She notices a large smudge of dirt on the slate. So she gets down on her knees and starts to scrub at it with a thick wire brush. It will not come off. She frowns and then starts to scrub harder and faster until the smudge finally disappears.

Once again up in the bedroom on the first floor, Kian throws back the bed covers, rips off the bedsheets, and inspects the mattress carefully.

Kian runs the taps for a while in the bathroom, then squirts cleaner into the large old four-claw bathtub and scrubs ferociously at it with a scouring pad.

Sun shines into the hallway as Kian sprays and wipes the staircase's handrail, working her way up and down with renewed enthusiasm. When she reaches the bottom, her thin body comes to rest, sitting on the bottom stair. She takes a deep breath, leaning over to open the Lighthouse front door, and stares out onto the landscape, admiring its beauty even though the dense rain clouds still linger.

Kian folds and bundles the bed covers and sheets into plastic garbage bags, ties them up, then stacks them tidily in the large old wardrobe. Kian lines her cosmetics and trinkets up along the dresser. On the chest of drawers, she places an old porcelain beautiful winged fairy doll. She dips into a suitcase and pulls out bed sheets still in their sealed packets. She makes the bed, then throws her quilt over the top of the bed, which now looks so much more inviting. She falls back, lying on it, enjoying the comfort of the old bed's new make-over. She stares up at the ceiling for the first time in a while, a slight smile slides across her face.

As the sun sets and the last rays of light fall, Kian outside in the semi-darkness empties all the used containers of cleaners along with the scouring pads and cleaning cloths into a garbage bag, ties it up then tosses it into the rubbish bin.

She comes back inside and, peering out from the window, watches the last rays dissolve as the night sky emerges littered with twinkling stars peeping through some of the dense dark clouds that still float across the night sky. Her face is more relaxed, deep in thought. Kian pulls her phone out of her jean pocket, flips the lid, pondering for a moment as her finger hovers over a letter on the keyboard. A tear or two swells up then she suddenly decides to quickly shut down the flip top and puts her phone back into her pocket.

Kian lights all the candles, which creates a beautiful enchanting atmosphere throughout the Lighthouse. She goes back to the large old armchair and sits down, nibbling on some dry biscuits, and looks around, admiring the changed, clean surroundings. She's exhausted now from a hard day's work and a job well done.

Three

Kian decides to take a bath. The classical music cascades throughout the Lighthouse, creating a calming atmosphere as she soaks in the hot steamy water. Relaxing back into the tub amidst the bubbles, she flicks her very long straight black hair back over the edge of the back of the bath, places her hand over her stomach, reaches over and grabs the large long, stem glass, and slowly sips her red wine, singing out aloud.

As the night air descends throughout the Lighthouse, she climbs out of the bath and dresses in her bathrobe. Kian wanders through the candlelit surroundings and switches off the CD Player. An eerie silence instantly descends upon the Lighthouse. It's deafening; she quivers for a second, deciding to turn the music back on immediately for reassurance, only this time on a much lower volume. Kian slowly climbs into bed, rolls over, and stares at her fairy doll atop the chest of drawers.

Outside, the sound of the howling wind grows louder, and the crashing waves become more profound. Then creaking noises, lots of spooky sounds as the house settles in the night. Kian, on edge, rolls over and hits the volume button on the CD Player, turning the music up slightly even higher. The classical music plays louder to drown out the strange background sounds. Relaxing again, Kian reminiscing smiles softly at her fairy doll, then closes her eyes.

The Lighthouse is lit by the bright rays of the morning sun again. Kian wakes, shaking her head searching for her watch to check the time. She sits up and opens the window, breath-ing in the vital sea air. She sighs for a moment, slowly curling up back on the bed, drifting off to sleep, bathed in the sun-shine coming through the window and warming her face.

Kian's cell phone rings! Kian's eyes open slowly. She fumbles for the phone, grabs it, and checks it. The caller ID reads: "JASON." The time reads: "7 a.m." Kian turns off the phone and rolls over, still half-asleep.

Suddenly her eyes snap back to attention. She jumps out of bed and stares in disbelief. Her fairy doll now sits at the foot of the bed. Kian cautiously approaches the fairy doll. She stops, looks around the room. She picks up the doll, inspects it, puts it back down, and looks around again. She moves back over to the window and gazes out at the ocean on edge.

It's late morning, and the fairy doll is propped up on the window ledge. The kettle boils, piercing the atmosphere of the kitchen. A spoon stirs a steaming coffee. Kian takes the cup in her thin hands, sipping on her first coffee for the day.

But her eyes and mind are fixed on the fairy doll. Kian snaps out of her train of thought, deciding to explore the Lighthouse surrounding her. Dressing quickly, she ventures outside and goes to the clifftop. She takes a sip of coffee then watches the waves lashing the rocks below.

As she studies the rugged coastline, she looks down towards the small coastal village in the distance. She's curious and races back up to the Lighthouse. Seagulls fly in flocks high above her.

Four

Kian's car motors slowly along the quiet street as the wind blows off the sea. She drives cautiously down the village's streets, where the roads lead, as the town is so unfamiliar to her. Kian views several small shops and sees a grocery store. She pulls into the car park, gets out, then grabs a trolley on her way through the grocery store doors.

After shopping and packing the groceries into her car, Kian sees a new-age bookstore across the road with a creatively painted sign over the door, and the placard reads, "MALACHIM." Intrigued, she crosses the road, peers in through the window, and decides to go in. A brass bell over the door rings as Kian enters. The building is historic, extravagantly eclectic, and crammed with bookcases and all types of books. Kian looks around. She pulls out a book, "SPIRITUAL HEALING," flips through it, then slides it back. She continues to run her fingers and eyes along row after row of old books with titles such as "TAROT MADE EASIER," "CELTIC MYTHS AND LEGENDARY TALES," and "THE LANGUAGE OF SYMBOLS THROUGH TIME."

She stops dead in her tracks. Oscar Prine, in his late

sixties, a man with dark glasses and a walking stick, is seated in the corner.

He acknowledges Kian's presence with a nod and a smile and says, "Hello, young lady."

Before Kian has time to react, someone else from the shop's backroom suddenly emerges and stands behind the large wooden antique counter in front of her. "Hello, Kian." She turns to see a handsome man in his late twenties smiling at her. This is Toby Harper, part-owner of the bookstore. Kian stares at him, a little stunned by the fact that he called her by her name. He sees her defense field come up and uses charm to calm her. Intrigued, he asks, "It is Kian, isn't it?"

In a defensive tone, Kian snaps back, "Excuse me." With a broad open smile that melts Kian's defense wall in a heart-beat. Curious about how Toby knows her name, assertive she asks, "Do I know you?" Charismatic in his response, he gently points to the elderly gentleman and lets Kian know that the elderly gentleman knows who she is. How does the elderly gentleman know her name? she inquires. No one responds to her question.

Unable to drop the matter, she probes further, "I beg your pardon." Toby senses that Kian feels exposed and attempts to soothe her nerves. Toby explains that they know she is a Kindergarten Teacher and has temporarily moved into the old Lighthouse on Wolf Rock while on her hiatus to write her bestseller novel. Stunned by Toby sharing this information, she demands to know how they knew this. Toby smiles again, indicating the new age surroundings. In a warm, sensitive tone, Toby introduces himself to Kian, "Toby Harper, local Clairvoyant." He reaches out to shake her hand, and as he touches her thin, cold, shaking hand, he draws close to Kian. For a moment, she is overwhelmed by his presence and stares into his large light blue captivating eyes.

Kian stands staunch, reeling by Toby's statement. She is mesmerized by Toby and unnerved by the elderly gentleman's cheeky display. A chubby little friendly aristocratic woman in her mid-sixties steps out from the back room carrying a stack of Books. This is Hetta Vandameer. Hetta, aware of Kian's nervousness, speaks very kindly, "They're toying with you, dear."

Hetta dumps the Books down on the large ornate antique reading table near one of the large tall bookshelves and frowns at Toby and the elderly gentleman.

Hetta scolds them both with tongue in cheek, "You two should be ashamed of yourselves. Acting as if you've never seen a pretty woman before." The elderly gentleman chuckling, banters playfully with Hetta, "I haven't." With his eyes still closed, the elderly gentleman sits patiently waiting for a quick response from Hetta. Flirting with the elderly gentleman, Hetta giggles and responds right on target with her quick wit. "Settle down you."

Kian, innocent and blushing, searches Toby's face for answers. Hetta explains to Kian that the Rental Agent had told them.

The Rental Agent was concerned that a young woman would be at the Lighthouse on her own. She had let them know to look out for Kian's welfare. Toby flashed a cheeky grin, proffered his hand. "It's terrific to meet you, and we're here if you need any help." Kian then shakes his hand again.

This time she is far more relaxed as she responds with a, "Likewise. I think?"

Hetta takes Kian aside and explains that she is the local historian. Hetta slaps the pile of Books she is carrying. With aristocratic pride, she pulls up a thick hardcover book with the front cover displaying large gold letters "By Hetta Vandermeer." Hetta introduces Kian to the blind gentleman sitting in the corner, her very dear friend and partner, Oscar Prine. Kian shakes Oscar's hand and introduces herself to him. He responds to Kian in a lovely warm well-spoken English gentleman tone.

Hetta gently pulls Kian away from Oscar and closer back to her as she discretely whispers in Kian's ear, "He was born as blind as a bat, but careful, he can see more than any of us ever will."

Toby gives Kian an admiring up and down. Toby now curious questions Kian about being a writer. Kian corrects Toby, explaining that she is an aspiring writer but has not been published yet. Toby, currently interested, responds, "What do you want to write?" Kian tells him she would like to write a children's book if she can get past her writer's block.

Hetta, on hearing Kian's statement, immediately jumps into the conversation; very confidently, Hetta speaks gently, "writers' block? I'm afraid there's no such thing, dear." Kian, surprised, responds with a questioning look at Hetta as if to say, "Really." Hetta, with worldly wisdom, continues with her following sentence. "Of course. Having nothing to write means having nothing to say." Kian smiles, nods politely, trying to mask her awkwardness. Hetta imparts more information to help Kian, "I don't suffer from it." Hetta waves her hand in the direction indicating her pile of books on the antique table. "Not since I tapped into this." Hetta slides the beautiful hardcover book across the sizeable antique table to Kian.

Kian, impressed and keen to explore this edition, further picks up the book, checking out the gorgeous calligraphy Gold writing on the front cover: "THE ANCIENT ART OF AUTOMATA" by Hetta Vandermeer.

Kian frowns skeptically, speaking out aloud. "Automatic writing?"

Looking into Kian's eyes, Hetta launches into a detailed account of her past conversations when meeting many famous authors and sharing their stories with her of how they write and what happens when they sit down to write and create their masterpieces. With renewed energy, Hetta continues naming some of THE most famous Writers. Oscar enjoys listening to the resonance of Hetta's voice and her captivating storytelling. This time Oscar interrupts in unison, sharing in the excitement, "The good ones, anyway." Hetta quizzically looks at Kian and asks, "Where do you think their inspiration comes from?"

Kian, feeling exposed again, cases the Bookshop seeking an invisible answer, then hesitantly taking a deep breath, gears up to answer, "The spirit world?" In turn, Kian is blown away by Hetta's response, "Absolutely. Inspiration is as infinite as death. It's just a matter of tapping the source."

Kian goes to hand the book back to Hetta. Kian hesitates to take the book and pushes it back to Hetta. Toby gently touches the book and pushes the book back toward Kian's stomach. His happy demeanor is eminent, "Tell you what...give it a try." Toby's enchanting smile entices Kian. "If it doesn't work, I won't charge you for it."

Kian smiles back and debates whether to accept the challenge. Toby backs up the challenge by adding a question to convince her. Kian continues standing glued to the spot, admiring Toby's handsome features as she regards the offer. Toby watches on with a gallant smile as she slips the book into her large leather tote bag.

Kian waves goodbye to them all, and she quickly leaves the bookstore. Astounded by her thoughts, Kian tried to quell her flirting behavior. Unsure of what just happened and what had come over her.

Five

Kian enters the Lighthouse carrying the bags of groceries. She takes out Hetta's book, smiles at it, and then tosses it onto the sideboard. She stares through the large kitchen window and looks out as the sun begins to cascade down through the orange sky and slip gently into the blue, blue ocean. Sunset reigns for a moment, then the night sky overwhelms the expanse, and twinkling stares begin to develop across the expansive universe.

Inside the warm Lighthouse, Kian sits eating a bowl of pasta and sipping wine. Her mobile rings. The ID reads, "JASON." Kian frowns debates with herself about answering it. She finally flips the phone open and listens. Jason's distressed, hurt voice over the phone is so clear, desperate, he pleads with her. "Kian?" Kian remains silent. Jason pleads again over the phone, "Talk to me... please?" But Kian continues to listen, and the silence is deafening. Jason explains to Kian how worried he is and that he has found all her medication in the rubbish bin at her home. He prattles on in his fear of losing her.

Kian does not react, as he repeatedly asks her what is going on and how she is feeling emotionally.

A long silent pause, then Jason, distressed on the phone, tries to persuade her to talk, to at least say something. "Please, honey. I need to know, please? Are you okay?" Kian finally, in a meek timed voice, speaks, her eyes well, activated by the doom of her rapid mood decline, "I wanted to feel alive again. I felt like my soul died when the baby died".

A shift takes place in Jason's tone. A sense of relief that he has gotten through to Kian, that perhaps he may be able to heal the conflict between them. He reassures Kian tenderly, "I know, honey. I know." Kian, although apprehensive, voices her feeling of liberation. "I'm happy now." Jason, still grappling for resolve, softens his tone even more. "Great, that's great, honey. Just tell me where you are, and I'll come to you. We can talk."

Kian falls silent again and on guard. Now very emotional and breaking down, Jason is talking over the top of her to try and win her affection back.

"It was never your fault. Never...." Tears form in Kian's eyes as Jason continues, "I've thought about what I said ... how I hurt you ... every minute of every hour of every day since you left. Please, honey. Please forgive me. Come back ... I love ---"

Unable to bear the emotional pain, Kian flips the phone shut with her frail, shaking hand then starts to weep.

Six

It's a new day, and Kian sits in front of a laptop and stares at it. Then she rolls her neck and shoulders, cracks her knuckles, and taps her fingers on the computer, then sighs, waiting for something to happen. Nothing does. She takes a deep breath and readies herself. No thoughts come for her to write. She closes her eyes with frustration and looks to the air for inspiration. Nothing comes. The day marches on with swiftness. The clock suddenly seems loud, striking the new hour. Kian checks her watch still no inspirational thought for her to write on the blank page.

Another hour slips by as Kian sits at the old table with a cup of coffee and her laptop, still staring at the Lap Top Screen. Unaware, for some time, she has been tapping her fingers on the table, straining to think. Growing restless, she begins to search for some food to eat. Seriously intense in her thoughts, Kian spoons ice cream from a container, so intent on thinking, she is not aware of the salted caramel vanilla ice cream taste and how much she is consuming.

The storm clouds begin to condense in the sky outside the large kitchen window, and the beginning of an orange-pink sunset manifests. As time moves on, Kian remains in the same spot at the large kitchen table, staring at the laptop blank screen. She notices a smudge on the screen. She gets up, goes to the pantry, pulls out some cleaning fluid, and cleans the laptop screen to distract herself.

Hours pass by as Kian has now given up on her laptop. She doodles on a writing pad instead. She stops, taps her pen on the table. As she looks at the window, she now notices the darkness outside. She sees the fairy doll still propped against the window. Kian gets up, takes the fairy doll in her thin fingers. Kian adjusts its dress, wings, preens its red hair, then pops it back against the window. She gazes out the window to the sea and the tumultuous dark world outside. For a moment, as she opens the window, she hears the roar of the crashing waves against the monolithic rocks below. She closes the window again, shudders, checking the time once again. She yawns, realizing it's now 2.00 am, and she decides to give it up for the night. In the still of the night, she wearily climbs the creeping stairs that echo through the stillness of the lonely Lighthouse up to the first floor, and in the dim light, she enters the room, the door slams shut. She turns suddenly, not realizing in her weariness that she slammed the door so firmly. She checks her thin arm and feels her bicep. She looks at it and frowns, then falls on the bed drifting into the realms of deep sleep.

A new day has come, and Kian looks well-rested, sitting outside on a blanket atop the cliffs near the monolithic rock formation, silhouetted against the low-lying sun. As she takes in the beautiful scenery, she hopes for some inkling of inspiration to activate her writing thread.

Kian suddenly cowers as A VOICE whispers on the wind, "Kian... Kian." She looks around, scouring the landscape as the voice calls her name.

Kian stands up, turning to the voice, back up to the Lighthouse. She grabs all her things, hurriedly bundling them in her arms. Fear sets in, her eyes dart frantically, casting side to side at the top of the Lighthouse. Something is on the balcony. Kian strains to see in the late-afternoon light. But all she can make out is just a dark shape. Everything suddenly goes quiet. No thundering surf. No squawking seagulls. No wind, just an eerie silence. The SHAPE dissolves. As Kian stands transfixed by the power of the Lighthouse, someone touches her on the shoulder. She jumps back and spins around, startled to see what is there. Losing her balance, she swiftly counteracts herself to regain her posture. It's Toby, "Sorry, didn't mean to spook you."

Kian, regaining composure, snaps. "What are you doing here?" Toby tries to reassure her with humor and, in a smooth as velvet tongue, speaks, "I forgot to tell you about the special offer. Kian caught left of center smiles, then blushes, "Offer?" Toby smiles back. Kian, for a moment, observes the sun shining directly on his attractive brown muscled body.

She looks away quickly, trying not to stare as he speaks, "Yeah, for this week only, every customer of mine gets..." Toby holds up a gift basket of cheese, crackers, and wine. "A free picnic for two," Kian chuckles, amused by his flirtation. The beautiful sunset is a remarkable sight today, and the sun's warm rays have warmed her up. The bottle of wine is empty. The crackers and cheese, half-eaten Kian and Toby relax to a glorious clear sunset. Kian acknowledges the picturesque landscape and appears happy with Toby's company as he chatters away, sharing his thoughts, "Sometimes I think about going back to the rat race and publishing, but then I look at this view." Toby breathes in the air and then admires the view. Kian nods to agree with his expression of thought. Toby probes Kian about her life in general and what has brought her to the Lighthouse. For a moment, Kian tries to brush off the questions.

For a moment, sadness washes over her face. She pulls a quick smile to compensate and hide her feelings. Kian takes a deep breath and stares out at the ocean. Toby waits patiently for an answer, aware he has hit on a nerve. Kian doesn't answer and sits in silence. Toby senses her awkwardness and makes a joke, "That bad, huh?" Kian still doesn't respond and prefers to deflect any attention away from her. Toby gently determined to discover more about her, "Okay, let's skip the past. What about the future? Any plans?"

Kian's response surprised by her play on words and her ambiguous, out-of-character response as she sits gazing out at the ocean, "My plan is, I have no plan." Kian bursts out laughing as Toby joins in with her infectious laugh. Toby charmingly nods and responds to her, "Okay, cool."

For the first time in an exceptionally long time, Kian is feeling liberated and empowered, then she turns and smiles and looks back up at the Lighthouse. She asks Toby who the owner is of the Lighthouse. He is knowledgeable on the Lighthouse topic but not aware of who owns the historic Lighthouse. He quips quickly, "Don't know. The Lighthouse was turned into a guest house after the shipping lanes were diverted to another location in the early seventies."

Kian expresses how beautiful she feels the place is. Even when in a storm and gale, she feels its beauty is breathtaking and enigmatic. Her passion for talking about it seems to lift her positively. Toby gazes at her. Kian suddenly becomes aware of him giving her a beguiling stare. "What?"

Toby plays the spiritual card. "I feel we have such a strong energy connection. I feel like I have met you before." Kian laughs, almost mocking him, "Oh, please."

Humoring her again with his warm, charismatic charm to quell her defensiveness, "No, no. You know what I mean." Kian remains practical, warding off any potential misunderstandings and remaining in denial about her awareness of finding him attractive. She sharply responds, trying to hide her physical interest. "No, I don't!" Toby attempts to convince her as he becomes deeply immersed in metaphysical concept analysis. "People connect sometimes. It's that instant energy connection and feeling, you know?" Kian poses the question back to him, questioning his belief system in a gentle probing way. Toby defended his position, trying to convince her with his statement, "Absolutely, even if they don't understand the energy, they feel it. It's something they can't explain".

Impulsively Toby stands up. He points to indicate the monolithic rock formation and immediate area. His belief in the words he speaks is so convincing. Kian stares into the pools of his blue eyes, his voice smooth, "Just like the energy that attracted us here to this very spot." Kian, suddenly keen to spend more time with Toby, wants to know more about this spot where they are standing and what's so special about this Lighthouse and its heritage and background.

Toby sits back down. He slides up close to Kian, who

draws her attention back up to the Lighthouse. Toby speaks slowly and softly in a captivating storytelling tone, "It's stood there for almost a hundred and forty years. Its light flashing thirty miles in every direction." He uses his hand and fingers to mimic each pulse of light magically. "First once, then one... two... three... four times, and finally, one—two—three, always repelling ships from danger." He flashes a knowing smile, adding, "Yet attracting lovers to this place." He pauses theatrically. Kian is now absolutely fascinated by his story-telling and feeling his warm body close to her side. He continues, "Couples would come here, and the Lighthouse would help them."

Kian frowns upon questioning his last statement. Toby observes her curiosity and continues with the conversation. "To say what they longed to hear from each other." Kian now stiffens, confused by his words. Toby continues to try to convince her.

He moves closer, looks her straight in the eyes, then, using his hand and fingers again to accentuate the 1-4-3 pulse of the Lighthouse signal, he slowly spells out, "I -- l...o...v...ey...o...u. Kian sits there feeling like she is falling into his eyes. A warm smile slowly forms across her face. She can't help but be impressed by his style. Toby sensually gazes at her, although he does not move. Then suddenly he stands and explains he must go as he has an appointment. The moment fragments between them. The intense dark shadow appears at the top of the Lighthouse as the clouds begin to gather swiftly in the backdrop. The breeze cools as Kian walks back up to the Lighthouse. She stops for a moment and watches Toby walking confidently in the distance back down to the village. She takes in the vital sea air. Her senses are on a high.

As the night air rolls in outside, Kian presses "play" on her CD player. Romantic classical music fills the interior of the Lighthouse. Kian has moved all her writing tools up to the next floor of the Lighthouse and made a makeshift study. The table sits directly in front of the large window, looking out onto the ocean. Kian is warmed up by the coffee, makes herself comfortable, and sits down with her laptop. The wind howls in the darkness outside. Kian looks excited as she views the blank screen. Then she types something slowly. ON THE LAPTOP SCREEN: The words: "I--- L-O-V-E --- Y-O-U." Kian savors this for a moment and smiles endearingly. Then she deletes it.

The large clock ticks on, moving the hands forward. Kian stands to stretch, then steps out onto the windy balcony and looks out into the darkness. The waves cascade in unison tonight, mesmerizing her gaze for an unknown time. She breaks her trance and goes back inside to her laptop. She attempts again to write.

The screen is still blank, and she has not written one word. Kian switches off the laptop. She's disappointed.

Seven

It's the middle of the day, and Kian sits at the kitchen table with a bottle of wine. Crumpled balls of paper are scattered on the floor. She scribbles something onto a writing pad in frustration.

She looks at it. She rips out the page, tosses it over her shoulder, sighs, and leans back, and yells, "Shiiiiiiiiiit!!!! She gets up, paces about, rolling her shoulders and neck. The air is chilling, and she grabs her large sweater to put on. She closes the window now that darkness has fallen. Kian forages for food to eat in the fridge, rubbing her neck and groaning. Slamming the fridge door shut, loudly she yells, "Shit! Shit! Shit!" Out of the corner of her eye, she glimpses Hetta's abandoned book sitting on the kitchen sideboard.

Kian lights a long thick candle places it on the kitchen table. Kian sits down with Hetta's Book and flips through the pages. On the last page is an old sepia-tone photo of a woman, late thirties, sitting at a table with a pen and paper, beneath the headline, "ROSEMARY BROWN – AUTHOR or WITCH?"

Kian looks at the photo then flips forward to a diagram

of a Yogi, sitting cross-legged beneath the Bodhi Tree Of Life with his aligned chakra points represented by colored dots aligned on specific points of his body.

Kian studies the diagram carefully and continues to flip through the pages. Later as the night passes on, the candle is almost burnt out, and the bottle of wine is now empty. Kian stares at the book, reading more and thinking deeper as she flicks the pages. Impulsively she shuts the book, closes her eyes, and takes a long deep breath, then whispers, "I now experience my Crown Chakra opening. I allow myself to be a channel for my Spirit Guide."

A long beat of silence reigns. Then the candle flickers. Kian sits perfectly still, soaking up the atmosphere, waiting for something to happen. Slowly she opens her eyes. She rolls her neck around, picks up the pen, and scrawls onto the writing pad, "Who am I speaking to?" Before she has time to think, her hand begins to write, "OSSIAN." Her eyes are fearful and widen as she sits bolt upright in her chair. Now falling into intrigue, Kian whispers the words as she writes them, "Ossian? Is that a woman's name? Her hand scrawls a response, "AS YOU SAY." Kian excitedly chuckles as she continues writing, "So, when do we start writing?"

Kian waits for a response. No reply. Kian shakes her head and mutters, "How do I know I'm not just talking to myself?" A beat, then her hand scrawls again, "YOU ARE NOT ALONE." Kian looks up at her fairy doll still planted on the kitchen window ledge, stopping again to think before she writes, "Where are you from?" "HERE." Stunned, Kian purses her lips and writes, "What do you want?" No reply. Kian, nervous, scribbles a question again. "Who are you?" Still no reply. Now a little annoyed, Kian vigorously underlines her last question.

"I said, who are you?" Still nothing. Silence reigns through-out the dim eerie Lighthouse. Kian looks up into the dark. The wind suddenly strikes loudly at the window. Kian is now angry at herself, "This is crap!" She hurls the writing pad across the room and storms out. She throws herself on the bed and punches the pillow a couple of times, swearing to herself. She lays there for a moment, then turns over, staring at the ceiling in the dark. Exhausted, she falls asleep in her clothes.

It is the dead of night. The rain beats down wildly as Kian sleeps. The window rattles in the rising wind. The stygian shadow creeps closer to Kian's face as she sleeps peacefully. Then, without warning, Kian sits bolt upright! Twitching vio-lently, but with her eyes still shut! Kian begins experiencing a vision.

Somewhere back in time. Pelting rain and howling wind. A muscular arm raises a Clan Clad Sword for an attack. A woman's weak hand reaches up defensively and screams for mercy. But the Sword slices down at her.

Kian's eyes fly open. She flings back the covers. She jumps out of bed and rushes out of the bedroom.

Kian pulls open the refrigerator door, rummages through the contents with trance-like intensity, spilling food all over the floor until she finds it, a bottle of cranberry Juice! Then she raids the pantry, finally finding a bag of peanuts!

Kian presses "repeat play" on a CD player. Music fills the Lighthouse again.

Kian grabs the pen and writing pad and sits on the floor.

Suddenly she goes all rigid. Her eyes glaze over as if in a catatonic state.

Then she begins to scribble onto the pad with a newfound velocity and vacant expression, effortlessly churning out page after page, utterly oblivious to everything around her. and slurping cranberry juice and gorging peanuts. Tossing completed pages over her shoulder and onto the pile on the floor, page after page, after page, hour after hour, after hour into the early hours.

It's now early morning, and the sunlight streams brilliantly through the window. Music still plays. Kian, her clothes now stained with cranberry Juice, is still writing frantically as if in a manic state. The juice container and the bag of peanuts are empty, and the floor is littered with pages of her frenzied manuscript writing. Suddenly, Kian stops writing. She falls back, her hand still clutching the pen and trembling for more. Her eyes blink rapidly. She drops the pen and looks around the room in confusion as if waking from a sleepwalk.

She sees the pages all over the floor. Curious, she picks up a page and starts to read. It's good, so good that she rummages through the pile until she finds the next page in sequence and continues reading. She chuckles in disbelief, overwhelmed by what she's read. She sits deep in conscious reality, trying now to recap the events of the night. Her thoughts are fragmented as she tries to piece together how she had written like that. Unfathomably she sits back on the floor. She moves into a downward dog yoga pose to stretch her back out.

Eight

A loud knock on the door startles Kian back to reality. She swiftly regains composure and heads to the front door. Now pale and bleary-eyed, Kian cautiously heaves open the door. Toby is standing patiently on the other side. He smiles, happy to see Kian as he holds up a bag of freshly-baked croissants. "Ah!! For your morning pleasure." Kian sweetly smiles as she invites him in. Toby notices her disheveled state. "What've you been up to?"

She points to the large pile of papers strewn across the floor, and she hands Toby the first page to read. Toby begins to read the page. Instantly fascinated by the content, he grabs the next page then sits comfortably, legs crossed on the floor, devouring Kian's manuscript.

Kian enters, now freshly showered and robed. Toby is too absorbed to notice her. Kian, pleased with herself, and his re-action to her manuscript, sensuously stretches out on the sofa and watches him devouring her words. He finishes reading the last page and gazes at her. Kian asks inquisitively, "What do you think?" He shakes his head and says, "WOW, it's brilliant. It's strange, but I know these feelings, and these words, it's like I've heard them before." Curious to know more, Kian responds, "What do you mean? You think I stole ... He comes close and puts his finger on her lips. She settles down by his tender action. Toby continues, "No, no, that's not what I'm saying." He picks the pages back up. He runs his fingers slowly along the page. "... it's like a beautiful lullaby ... sung to you as a child ... and hearing it again as an adult." Kian sits bolt upright, now trying to fathom his words, and validate her work. "That's good, isn't it?"

She searches his handsome face again for answers. "No, not good, brilliant." Kian giggles with child-like delight as he adds to his bold statement, "A sure-fire masterpiece! As he collects all the pages up and assertively continues his sentence. "And I know just the person to give it to."

Kian, suddenly feeling insecure, resisting his confident appeal, "Doesn't matter! Once they get a hold of this, there's going to be a bidding war! Guaranteed!" He stands close to her, holding gently onto her thin arms and sensuously winks, pointing to the book on automatic writing. He warmly teases her, "Looks like you owe me." Kian denies the book's help, "It had nothing to do with it." Toby laughs into the air. He is so close to her face now. Gleefully he challenges her, "Yeah?"

Kian breaks his hold and goes out to the kitchen as the kettle boils loudly. She was attempting to defend herself, her work, and her intelligence. "Every one of those words came from me, not one of your silly ghosts. "Toby is again sitting crossed-legged on the floor, re-reading the story's beginning filled with ideas and enthusiasm. She gets up and comes up behind him. She kisses him softly on the neck, purring, "... I'm still hungry." She turns him around, facing him straight on, and then kisses him hard on the mouth. Toby is overwhelmed and backs away. He stares into the embers of her eyes, fighting his feelings and the moment. "I can't," he turns his head away.

Kian kisses him on the neck again. He breathes deep, closing his eyes, trying to fight the lust. He tries breaking the silent moment, "I just think you ought to know ... at the moment I'm..." Kian gently cups his face then adds, "You're with me." She pushes him back onto the couch playfully.

She slides on top of him. He closes his eyes, overcome by the stirring in his loins. Unable to resist her sensual touches on his bare smooth muscular, tanned skin, engulfed by the passion of the moment, he succumbs to her strong advance.

Late into the night, Kian stands on the porch in the dim light watching as Toby drives off into the night. Her face bore an alluring afterglow shining out from within. Contented, she leans up against the old lighthouse wall, daydreaming about the last few romantic hours. She can't remember how long it had been since she felt this alive.

Nine

Kian sits down in the candle-lit kitchen with a pen and pad at the table. Her mind wanders as she writes, "Ossian. I'm ready to continue." The silence is deafening. Kian continues writing on the pad, "Ossian. Are you there?"

Still, nothing happens. Kian tries to write her request differently without being so demanding, "I'm ready to continue now." A bolt of robust and intense energy rips through her feeble hand. Her hand suddenly scrawls, "I AM NOT."

As Kian sits in the candlelight, we see directly hovering behind her near the window the ethereal shadow hovering, observing Kian with great intensity, the eyes of the spirit raging with anger. Kian shudders as the goosebumps rise up the back of her neck. She quickly pens her next question to Ossian, "Why?"

No reply. Kian waits, unsure what's happened. Her own sudden guilt triggers her own paranoia. Kian becoming anxious, quickly writes, "What's wrong?"

Nothing happens. The dead of the night in the Lighthouse becomes eerie. Kian sighs, frustrated. She writes again on the pad. "What do you want?" Kian waits. Ossian replies:

The Dark Shadow moves closer to Kian as Kian's arm turns stiff. As she tries to write, the intense, uncontrollable energy suddenly runs through her arm. "A PROMISE." Kian is oblivious to the dark shadow hovering close by as she remains trying to solve the mystery. "Promise? From who?" Kian is fixated, waiting on a response. The writing response comes to Kian's surprise, "FROM YOU."

Kian quickly asks the question back, looking up in the air. I don't understand, "What do you want me to promise?" Kian's hand writes with unusual strength.

"A FAVOR." Kian hesitates, then curious to learn more, she stares at the Pad then quickly jots down her demanding question to Ossian, "What kind of favor?" Silence again. Kian, impatient again, writes in a challenging tone, "What favor, Ossian?" Ossian responds, "FIRST YOU MUST PROMISE." Kian sits rigidly on the chair, feeling cornered, unsure, and very suspicious of what appears to be some type of game.

Again Kian writes, "Tell me what you want first." Ossian is aware of Kian's impatience. Kian, unable to control her arm this time, reports, "DO YOU WANT TO FINISH OUR WORK?" For Kian, this is such an easy question to answer. She immediately writes, "Yes." Kian feels like her arm is moving by different energy, "THEN MAKE YOUR PROMISE WITH ME." Kian falters, thinks about it for a moment, reads the writing, then mutters, "This is nuts." But Kian's hand scribbles intensely again. "PROMISE ME."

Kian senses the demand is strong. Resistivity again Kian writes, "Not until you tell me what you want." A long silent beat. Then Kian angrily snaps, yelling at the walls, "What do you want from me!!" Then the reply channeled through her arm in the written words, "THE SAME AS YOU WANT FROM ME." Kian slumps back in her chair, shakes her head in frustration, then scribbles, "And what's that?" Her hand begins to cramp and scrawls, "FREEDOM." A beat as Kian regards the answer, the writing flows through Kian's arm uncontrollably, "DO YOU PROMISE?"

As Kian sits there gazing at Ossian's written request, Ossian reassures Kian, suddenly aware that Kian is becoming frightened, "NO HARM WILL COME TO YOU."

Kian regards the written words of Ossian. Wanting desperately to be that writer she had always wanted to be and to be a successful one at that, Kian whispers and then verbally commits, "...I promise."

Kian's handshakes as she scribbles, "IT MUST BE WRITTEN!!" Kian feels anxiety and that the opportunity could slip away.

Kian slowly writes with commitment: "I PROMISE." There is a long, deathly silence. All the candlelight throughout the Lighthouse starts to flicker and glimmer. Kian looks around the eerie surroundings, a little unnerved. Sensing a presence, without warning, it begins again. Kian's eyes glaze over. She sits up rigidly in her chair and hits 'play' on her CD player. And now, under Ossian's spell again, she continues to write as the music plays and Kian works away for hours. Kian sits on the sofa, engrossed with reading back over pages she has just written.

Many hours pass, she continues writing at an incredible speed into the night. Fixed, channeling the energy through as her hands write at a rate of knots.

The kitchen of the Lighthouse is now a mess. But an

unkempt-looking Kian still writes on, polishing off, page after page, as she continues to add them, one by one, to the pile on the kitchen table, oblivious to her surroundings and the turn of time.

Later that day, outside on top of the Lighthouse, Kian continues to scribble page after page, perched atop the balcony enjoying writing in the warm sun with beautiful serious clouds scattered across the solid blue sky, such a picturesque landscape to be in and so in her element. Her mind raced with the energy of the story being written.

Later that night, Toby visits, curious to know what Kian is up to. Caught up in the excitement of the rush, she leads him to the bedroom and pushes him onto the bed. Toby is off guard but goes with the passion of the moment. Surprised, Kian grabs pages of her writing and begins to read aloud to Toby. He gets comfortable and snuggles up, listening intently to every word of the story.

Ten

It's late at night, and Toby is now long gone. Kian is enjoying a bowl of pasta and wine while reading her new pages down in the kitchen. She appears content knowing Toby is in full support of her writing, her story, and her.

Her phone rings. She moves excitedly to answer it, feeling it was Toby again willing to share more good feedback about her story. Just before answering, she checks the caller ID. "JASON." She gasps, caught off guard. A sudden feeling of guilt distorts her pretty face. Immobilized temporarily, Kian stares at the phone, unsure for a second what to do, deciding to let the phone ring, her mind ticking over as it rings out. Abruptly she switches it off, feeling relieved. The music playing on the CD player suddenly stops.

An eerie vibe falls like a veil throughout the room. The silence is deafening. Kian, guilt-ridden, sits still glued as her mood now declines, her eyes begin to dance nervously as she scans the room. She calls out, "Hello ... is anyone here," "Ossian. Is that you?"

The fairy doll suddenly falls from the window behind. Startled, she races over and closes the large window, shutting out the chill of the wind and picking up the beautiful doll. She places the fairy doll back on the wide window ledge, admiring its beauty.

Her mood shifts once again, back to warm as she looks at the photo suddenly falling back into her love bubble, admiring the snapshot of Toby, which lay strewn amid all her written pages on the kitchen table. She yawns, takes the photo with her heading upstairs to bed.

It's early in the morning, a chill still in the air from the early morning dew, as the sunlight warms Kian up, disbursing its rays of warm, bright light down the cobbled street where she walks, dressed smartly, strolling along the road, window-shopping.

As she stands there, staring into a lolly shop window. A well-spoken mature male voice comes up from behind. "How's the writing?' Kian, surprised, spins around to see Oscar carrying a loaded shopping bag, wearing dark glasses, and using a walking blind stick. He beams at her as he taps her foot gently with his blind stick. "Young lady."

Kian responds endearingly as she greets Oscar. Kian looks around further. Oscar, sharp as a tack, "She's not here." Kian's face is now confused. Oscar comes swiftly back at Kian, "Hetta. I assume that's who you're looking for?"

Kian smiles at his uncanny ability. He holds up the heavy shopping bag. "She needed some tea and jam. Oscar takes a deep breath, "But now I'm afraid I've overdone it."

Kian offers out a reassuring respectful arm to help him, "Are you alright? She takes his arm, guides him over to a nearby bench. "Here, take a seat here on the bench." Oscar feels for the metal arm, then confidently sits himself down, catching his breath coming to rest on the Kings Bay English Victorian Old Style green metal bench placed right outside the bookstore.

True to his gentlemanly disposition, he thanks her for her kindness. Once again, Kian, unsure as to his physical self, asks after his health. He openly responds. "I'm afraid it's the combination of a weak heart and even weaker will." He reaches into his coat pocket, pulls out a small antique silver whiskey flask takes a quick sip. Kian, surprised by his actions, is concerned she questions Oscar. "Should you be doing that? Oscar, sweet and flippant, leans on his bind stick as he responds. "I suppose not." He takes another swig then adds with a charming schoolboy smirk. "But at my age, doing what you're not supposed to can make life just that little bit more interesting." For a second, Kian reminisces about Toby, and she agrees with Oscar, tongue in cheek. "I see!!!" Oscar chuckles as he somehow feels he has converted her as an ally. "Well, I can't." Oscar struggling to his feet continues, "And therein lays the dilemma that you might be able to help me with." Kian now willingly offers more assistance. Oscar stands tall and good-looks strong and apparent. "Would you be so kind as to escort me back home?" Kian offers her car to drive him home if he would prefer to travel that way.

Oscar cheekily inquires, "car?" Kian explains that her car is parked across the road. Oscar pushed the envelope, "Only under one condition." Kian startled, secretly thinking another condition she must resign herself to. Curious, she asks him what that may be. Oscar flashes an impish grin again. "That I will be allowed to drive, they both laugh heartily as Kian escorts Oscar toward her car.

Eleven

Kian's car motors along the sleepy, sunny seaside street nestled along the scenic route of Wolf Rock Point. Kian drives while Oscar entertains her with a story, detailing how he first met Hetta at the spiritual circle at the Pentecostal Church and how he can still remember her beautiful scent of Cinnamon. Oscar inhales deeply through his nose. He speaks in gentlemanly romantic fashion, "Sweet ... sensual ... cinnamon, like the most powerful of aphrodisiacs."

Kian, caught up in the moment in awe, responds." Sounds like love at first smell to me." Suddenly realizing what she said, Kian tries to backtrack quickly, avoiding appearing rude. Oscar smiles, knowing the irony of the words, and they share a laugh. Then, Kian, enthralled, asks him about herself. He explains that that was how he knew she was standing outside the shop today. Kian, surprised and very curious, asks, "What do I smell like?" To her surprise, Oscar comes back with a quick "That's easy, Disinfectant."

Kian looks at him, unsure as Oscar continues the conversation. "This vehicle reeks of it. So do you. I smelt it on you the first time we met. Most people I know, who have OCD, have this clinical smell about them, which I can smell. I don't know if others can smell this, though." Oscar continues explaining that he finds the OCD comes from past trauma of some sort. Oscar also shared his concern of hoping that Kian was O.K. as he reassured her, "and just to let you know my sweet. Al-though we have only been recently acquainted, Hetta and I are here if you need anything. Please do let us know."

Although very touched with a caring look in her eyes, Kian loses the smile and falls silent. Oscar senses the atmospheric shift and apologizes to Kian. Oscar, for a moment, now feeling he has offended her. Kian tries to hide her emotions and is glad that Oscar cannot see her tears swelling up, as Kian denies being offended, although the look on her face tells us another story. Oscar softens the resonance of his voice. Sweetly he asks, "What are you running from?"

Kian explains she isn't running from anything. Oscar shifts his intent to more of a spiritual one, "something follows you... haunts you. Something you are always trying to cleanse... to control." So sad and vulnerable, Kian gazes at the road ahead, deep in guilt. Oscar, caring, probes again, "What are you so obsessed with removing from your life?" Kian stares straight at him, about to confront him. Sensing the vibe, he flashes a caring, warm smile, catching Kian off guard. Once again, Oscar, with an uncanny knowing, perks up cheekily, "We're here."

Kian's car pulls into the driveway of a rambling 18th century historical house. The English rose adorned garden manicured to perfection. Kian scans the exquisite surroundings of the well-nourished hedges and statuesque waterfalls throughout the acreage area. Kian hops out of her car, helping

Oscar, who offers an olive branch and invites her into the sprawling mansion for a cup of English tea. Kian declines the invitation explaining she must get back to the Lighthouse. Dismayed that Kian wants to rush back to the loneliness of the old Lighthouse, she thinks about it again and decides to take up his invitation. The door clicks, and the door swings open. Kian follows Oscar inside. She cannot help but be impressed with the expensive antique furniture and historical paintings as she allows Oscar to take off his coat. Oscar shouts out as he hangs his coat and hat on the rack. "I have returned with a guest." He calls out, then faces Kian explaining, "She'll be so happy to see you."

Hetta gracefully enters, wearing an old designer purple paint-stained work coat and purple gloves. When she sees Kian, her face lights up, opting to greet Kian with a warm hug, "Hello dear," Hetta kisses Kian on the cheek. "What a wonderful surprise."

Hetta steps back and admiringly gives Kian the quick once over. "You're looking splendid. So much better than when we first met." Hetta gazes admiringly at Oscar's face for a brief second, "Isn't she just the picture of health?" Oscar ironically agrees, and Kian smiles as Hetta asks, "How long has it been now? Five, six weeks?"

Kian was mulling over the question for a second, stating, "it's almost four already." Hetta surprised, "A month? Already? My goodness dear, how time flies, and the book?"

Kian regards Hetta quizzically. Hetta is curious to know if Kian read Hetta's book, "Your bestseller from beyond." Kian humors Hetta as she happily shakes her head, acknowledging the contents of the book only slightly. Hetta, with an inquiring mind, probes Kian for more information, "Coming along well, no doubt?" Kian explains in a slow tone that the book is coming along slowly. Hetta beams with an admiring smile, driven by her inner knowledge.

Hetta turns to Oscar and asks him to put the kettle on and prepare some tea and scones for the three of them. Oscar happily obliges and wanders off toward the large expansive, light-filled kitchen. Hetta watches him leave, then turns to Kian, "Such an angel, that man. He will do anything for me, you know. And to think when I first met him, his only ambition was to be shot in the back by a jealous husband!" Kian laughs aloud with Hetta at the irony of her statement.

Hetta politely excuses herself to dash out of the room to wash up and change out of her painting clothes. Kian inquires after Hetta's large piece of opulent artwork sitting on the giant easel frame in front of her and what Hetta is currently painting. Hetta comes back with a quick response explaining that it's nothing special at present. The picture will evolve as she continues to work on it and that the result will come out of the colors, which will then create a basis and formation, then she will enhance the base of this to add on and complete the piece based on that. Hetta explains this is all part of her new collection that she is working on with a different intuitive approach.

Kian fascinated probes further, asking about Hetta's collection and if it is possible to see these works of art. Hetta is a humble tone explains that Kian will have to google them on the internet, as they are currently on show in the Families' New York Art Gallery. Kian is astounded by this and asks to see more of Hetta's work. Hetta guides Kian down the long stately hallway and into her studio. Kian saunters, absorbing all the treasures within the hallway, then comes to a halt, gazing at something with a mixture of fear and intrigue.

Stored in a row of jars are wax imprints of hairless human heads of different sex and ages and feet, hands and forearms. Some faces are pleasant, smiling, while others are spooky, disfigured with pain and anguish. Some have been meticulously brushed over with life-like tones, while others remain in their original ghostly white wax. It is macabre and scary, like a turn of the century freak show. The studio is crammed with molds, paint, and brushes. Kian doesn't know what to make of it. She stops at the workbench and stares at a half-painted head of a young girl, frozen in a horrifying scream. Kian, disturbed by the piece of work, quizzically looks to Hetta, "I don't understand. What are you trying to say with all this?" Hetta gently responds, "I'm not trying to say anything, dear," as Hetta waves her hand to indicate that this collection is channeled from the hereafter. Chills run up and down Kian's spine, and the goosebumps rise as she fearfully asks Hetta, "They're dead???" Hetta attempts to reassure Kian, "Not dead. There is no death." Hetta serene calmly walks around the room, admiring her eerie collection. "There is only another transition for some, like a change of clothing." Hetta searches Kian's face, unsure as to Kian's state of spiritual evolvement, "Some are fortunate enough to realize this."

Hetta stops by a mold that has a terrified expression. Pointing to the wax figure works, "While others, well, these poor souls are like shadows. They don't know they're dead or where they are, not yet, or at least not until I help them."

Kian, dumbfounded by Hetta's comment, quips, "Help them?" Kian is now scared.

Hetta, observing the fear rise in Kian's face, reassures Kian by reaching out to touch Kian's shoulder. Then with great sincerity, Hetta continues, "To pass over to their next dimension. The ones that are painted have passed now. They are complete, where they need to be. The others, I still have to help when they're ready to come to me." Kian, still dumbfounded but curious as well, wants to know how Hetta can see them. Kian's mind is racing with questions now. Hetta feels Kian's mental adrenaline rush, attempting to settle Kian's inquiring mind. "No. I'm what is known as a Clairaudient or a sensitive. They speak to me. Sometimes in languages, I don't even understand." A foreboding feeling washes over her pretty face. Kian is skeptical now and cross-examines Hetta. "I still don't get it. You say you can't see them." Hetta explains again that she is unable to see them. Kian, once again skeptical, asks, "Then how do you know what they look like?"

Hetta gently leads Kian by the hand into another beautiful large drawing room alight with sunlight and lush greenery. Hetta settles her into a blue Art Deco armchair. Kian sits. However, she remains reserved and unsure.

Twelve

In a conservatory full of exotic plants and wicker furniture, Kian listens to Oscar as Hetta pours tea. In his clear, sincere tone, he says, "It's my gift. I am a channel. They first appeared to me at an early age, all different shapes and ages and races. They felt like warm sun on my cold skin."

Reminiscing, he smiles softly, "I thought they were angels come to light my darkness." Kian, emotionally engaged, quips, "So the molds? You made them?" Oscar responds, clarifying the matter, "No. They did."

Kian's expression of confusion slides across her face, so she turns to Hetta, seeking more clarity to the question she has asked Oscar. Hetta quickly answers and shares the metaphysical information, "they're formed during a physical séance." Generally, we use a dish of warm quick setting wax." Enthusiastic, Oscar cuts into the conversation, explaining even more about the spiritual procedure that he and Hetta use. "Then we invite the materialized spirit to show itself or dip into it. The wax will rapidly begin to set, then we are left with an impression of the Spirit who has come through to us."

Kian sips from her Royal Dalton teacup as she shoots

them an unsure, skeptical look. Hetta appearing to be understanding of Kian's skepticism reassures Kian. "It's alright, dear. Most people think we're quite mad."

Kian glimpses two prominent vertical scars across Hetta's wrist as Hetta pours some more tea. Kian ponders the wounds, but Hetta doesn't notice Kian has noticed and moves on with her wise words to reassure Kian that they are not as insane as she may currently be thinking. "But, as the poet once said, 'farewell to the known and exhausted." Oscar leans forward and adds with a loving knowing smile, "... and welcome to the unknown and illimitable ..."

Kian, slightly shaking from nervousness as she tries to hide her fear, smiles sweetly at Oscar and Hetta. Kian explains that she must head off before it gets too dark, so she can find her way back quickly to the Lighthouse. They warmly escort Kian to the front door, and in a warm embrace, they part ways, and she drives off into the gorgeous sunset.

Kian still unnerved by the whole conversation with Hetta and Oscar; which has not sat comfortably with her, analyzing to the ninth degree, as she mulls it over and over while driving along the rugged terrain, back up the road to the iconic historic Lighthouse, and the safety of its haunting confines.

Thirteen

Kian lies next to Toby. They are asleep in each other's arms. Outside, the wind howls, the rain beats down hard, and lightning fires attacks across the dark sky again and again. Kian, disturbed by the loud-sounding cracks, opens her eyes. In the dim light, she smiles as she looks across at the sensuous sleeping Toby. Then she slides softly and quietly out of bed. She goes to the window, standing restfully. She gazes outside, staring out into the abyss of the storm-filled darkness, feeling amazed at how different she feels now in the warm afterglow compared to hours before in the depths of her deep empty despair.

A sudden intense flash of lightning reveals a dark shape floating in the corner behind her. Sharply Kian whips around, her arms covered with goosebumps. A chill rises swiftly up the back of her spine. She is instantly aware of something present, but the dark shape disappears immediately.

Kian steps back, unsure of what she just observed and sensed. Frantic, she surveys the room then looks at Toby, still fast asleep. She checks out the window again, nothing there, nothing at all.

She goes back to bed. However, restless and unable to sleep and so on edge, she decides to head down to the bathroom and shower to relax. She tries not to wake Toby in the early morning hours and creeps around as quietly as possible. Kian turns on the hot water, steps into the shower cubicle, and enjoys the warm water flowing over her.

Toby seems contented as he continues to sleep soundly on his back. Kian is now downstairs enjoying the hot shower, shrouded in steam. Kian begins to relax as the steam starts to escape from the bottom of the cubicle. Rising like a cobra, it twirls out the bathroom door and now down the hallway. The thick steamrolls along the floor then snakes around the stair-case handrail, heading directly towards the upper level.

Toby still sleeps peacefully on his back. The thick fog-like steam floats into the bedroom and hauntingly lingers over Toby. It stops abruptly. Then in the twilight light of the room, the steam shape immediately turns the darkest shade of black.

It glides toward Toby's upper body and stops to hover directly above him. Suddenly the black fog gathers and rolls into A HUMAN LIKE SHAPE, no distinct features, just a dark outline. The dark shape floats down and squats lightly on the chest of sweet, unsuspecting Toby. It idles there for a moment before it lurches closer to Toby rolling its head from side to side in a curious fashion as it studies Toby's face. It raises an arm, and black steam seeps from its fingers. Then it slowly plunges its hand into Toby's open mouth. Toby suddenly starts gagging. His eyes fly open only to see A LARGE CLAN CLAD SWORD stuck in his stomach. Terrified, Toby gasps in horror. He immediately rolls from the bed and falls hard onto the floor. He moans, clutching his stomach. The Sword has vanished. Toby attempts to orientate himself. He shakes his head, thinking he must have been dreaming. In a panic, Toby feels on the bed in the dark for Kian. She is not there.

Frantic, he jumps up and dashes out of the room in the dark, stubbing his toe on the edge of the door. Toby jumps up and down on the spot, grimaces in pain, holding on to his big toe, attempting to ease the pain. Kian, dressed in her bathrobe, slowly makes her way up the stairs. Toby is panicking, quickly trying to dress as he scrambles down the staircase toward her. He scours the surroundings, not sure of what he's just experienced. Toby feels his chest, checking for the Sword, which has abruptly disappeared. He is stunned. Kian, concerned, rushes to soothe his nerves. Toby is freaking out, breaking out into a sweat. He hastily lets Kian know he must go. Half dressed, Toby runs toward the front door. Kian shoots him a suspicious look as he scurries further toward the front door.

Disturbed by his behavior, Kian probes as to what is going on for him, quietly wondering if he had seen the apparition she thought she saw. Kian asks, "Are you O.K?" Toby responds, still very shaken and anxious, "Yeah, yeah. Look, I gotta go." Kian doesn't believe him. Toby tries to validate his erratic behavior, "I've got something I need to do." He pecks her on the cheek, then evacuates irrationally through the front door, out into the torrential storm.

Kian stands fixed. Unsure what she has just witnessed, Kian peers out of the window, watching as Toby drives off like a wild maniac along the muddy Lighthouse driveway back up onto the main road.

Fourteen

It is the dead of night, and the wind and rain outside rally, thrashing at the walls of the Lighthouse harshly. Hours on, Kian, now comfortable, sprawls on the sofa, comfortably listening to angelic music, which creates an alpha ambiance through the Lighthouse. Deep in thought, she picks up her cell phone, flips it open, then switches it on. The phone beeps a couple of times, announcing new messages in her message bank. Kian opens the first message. It's from JASON, and it reads: "HELP ME TO HELP YOU. CALL ME."

Kian is looking serious studying the message. Then she selects "REPLY." Her thumb hesitates to rest on the "SEND" button. A crashing sound suddenly snaps Kian's attention directly towards the hallway. She moves swiftly, adrenalin rushing as Kian's thoughts scatter as she enters the hallway, only to find the window shutters open and banging in the wind. Breathing a sigh of relief, she quickly secures the shutters. Kian goes back to the living area. She stops suddenly, noticing something on the floor. She moves closer, her eyes widening with curiosity as she attempts to define what it is. She stands fixed, staring, now on the floor she sees trapped within the texture of the slate tile floor, swirling around is a Turin Shroud-like ghostly image of a face, its features barely discernible in its midst as the vision grows more robust, more transparent and more defined.

Kian shudders. She steps back in fear, away from where the apparition lay on the floor. She shakes her head, questioning her vision, wondering if this is just a figment of her imagination. Kian races to the kitchen and flings open the cupboard door beneath the sink, pulling out cleaning products and rubber gloves.

Kian is now on her knees, frantically scrubbing with a thick brush, trying to remove the haunting image from the slate floor. She stops, wiping away the cleaning fluid. The picture remains fixed, hauntingly staring at her.

Then she leans closer and slowly wipes the slate again. As she kneels there, a loud knocking on the door startles Kian, who quickly jumps to her feet. She approaches the door quietly, cautiously. Kian calls out assertively, "Who is it?" Hetta responds from the locked door with her warm, eloquent English tone, which bears a sense of urgency. "It's us, dear! Open up!"

Kian, relieved, quickly unlocks then heaves the door open. Hetta, Oscar, and Toby swiftly step in. Hetta carefully guides Oscar through the large door with a burst of wind and pelting rain. Kian, relieved and curious, "What are you doing here?"

Hetta instinctively brushes past Kian and walks around inspecting the Historic Lighthouse surroundings. She stops, working intuitively; she closes her eyes, senses her surroundings, feels the atmosphere, and deciphers the room's vibrations. Oscar leans on the safety of the wall, unfamiliar with his surroundings. Toby engaged completely on Hetta, trying to tune into what Hetta is sensing, agonizingly waiting for her to speak, "My goodness! Can you feel it?" Oscar closes his eyes for a moment and responds, "It's powerful, willful, and very feminine." Kian whispers to Toby, "What's going on?" Toby, always charismatic, smiles at Kian. "Don't worry. It's going to be fine." Hetta excited, chips in, "Yes, dear. We're here to help." Embracing Kian's arm and leading her around the room, observing the tile floor. Hetta leads the way, still looking everything over. Kian chases after her. Kian is unsure of what is happening and confused. "Can somebody please tell me what's going on"? Hetta reassures Kian and the others explaining that she needs information from Kian as to what Spirit she has unleashed in the confines of the Lighthouse. Kian, spun out in disbelief, and feeling defensive, responds, "Unleashed? What are they talking about?"

Toby respectfully looks at Hetta. She nods. So Toby begins to speak cautiously, explaining, "Tonight, upstairs in the bedroom, something attacked me. Oscar cuts into the conversation with precision, "Something angry ... unfulfilled!" Hetta then observes that Kian is not coping with the information they are imparting and regards Oscar, "Oscar, please. There's no need to scare her." Oscar, protective of Kian, explains that Kian needs to know. "For her safety." Kian's face turns to fury attacking them all with her words, "What the hell are you people talking about? Oscar jumps in once again to soothe her defensiveness. "Hetta's book. You used it, didn't you?" Kian, not sure what has happened, denies her position, "Of course not."

Hetta steps in to control the situation with caring support, "please, dear, we don't have time. You've used my book and inadvertently dredged up some poor soul with an agenda that seeks closure of some kind. Kian is biting back, wanting to know more. Hetta, sympathetic to Kian, once again reassures her that at this point, it may be nothing to worry about, but they must work together to resolve this spiritual matter, and all must be honest so they can prepare for what may come. As blind as he is, Oscar raises his eyes to the ceiling. His face speaks volumes of foreboding consequences that may come if they don't nip the situation in the bud. Hetta quietly glares at him. Oscar, sensing Hetta's face and thoughts, apologizes sincerely to all parties being the proper gentleman.

Hetta gently speaks directly to Kian, "Now, I'm not saying what you've released is necessarily bad. But we do need some clarification. Toby impatiently intervenes curiously, "We need to know what it is." Overwhelmed, Kian slumps down on the sofa and sighs, exasperated with nowhere to go. Kian realizes that she may need their help. Once again, Oscar cuts in, "We don't even know if it's male or female."

Kian looks at Hetta, then coyly at Toby, then deciding to come clean, slightly embarrassed she mutters, "It's female." Hetta questions Kian again, unsure what Kian has just said. Kian reiterates sternly that the Spirit is female. Oscar immediately seeks out proof from Kian, "How do you know?

Kian begins by telling the three that the Spirit's name is Ossian. Excited, Hetta jumps into the conversation again, "Ossian? Well, that is a start. Is there anything else we should know?"

A long beat of silence as Kian regards the question. The three patiently await Kian's following words to unravel more of the mystery. Kian suddenly goes into an enthralling story of how it all came about and how Ossian had made Kian promise. Oscar eerily intercepts, "You mean a covenant?" Oscar's mind is ticking over strategically assessing bullet points of Kian's story. Toby comes into the conversation again, inquiring what the promise was and what Kian has committed to. Kian naively explains it was in the form of a favor. Hetta, mesmerized and intensely intrigued, swoops in, "What kind of favor?"

Kian shoots back a defensive response, "It never said. All it wanted was my promise to deliver." Hetta, protective of Kian, inquires, "And this promise, it was in return for what?" Kian, becoming intolerant to all the questioning, sighs, "More pages?" Oscar says, "This is becoming very worrisome very quickly." Hetta looks into Kian's eyes, saying, "This manuscript you're writing with it, what it about, what type of genre is it?"

Toby intervenes again, full of admiration for Kian's manuscript, "It's a love story." Kian then adds to the storyline, "A tragedy set in the seventeenth century."

Hetta continues asking specific questions to actualize the current metaphysical situation. Hetta probes further to discover whether the Spirit is trapped in one room in a vibration vortex in the Lighthouse or not. For Hetta to work out a path forward to connect with the Spirit at the most vital point within the Lighthouse walls, she needs a contact point to work from. Hetta will contact the Spirit to discover why the Spirit has emerged and for what purpose. Hetta trying to soothe Kian, asks, "Which room do you do most of your writing in?"

Kian, still defensive, wants to know why Hetta asks all these questions. Hetta sits Kian down, explaining many things about the physic realms based on her years and years of experience with the metaphysical world. To help Kian feel comfortable understanding what may be at stake and perhaps shed some light on what is going on and what could happen. Oscar suggests they do a round-table channeling session to see if the four of them can communicate with Ossian, the Spirit, and get more insight into the Spirits' quest or purpose. Hetta explains to Kian to do this. First, they must prepare the room with good healing energy and create a positive space for the Spirit's energy to come through. Kian agrees and takes them to where she has been writing her manuscript and thinks back to when the channeling seemed to be the strongest. Hetta begins to prepare, ordering Toby to mop the floor and clean the table with sage. They burn white sage in all four kitchen corners and shift the larger round wooden table into the kitchen area. Toby goes out to his car, brings back some clearing and cleansing aromatherapy oils, and sets them up in Kian's oil burner. He places a large amount of wax in a glass cooking container on the stove and heats up the mass of wax, so it is slightly melted, and then places this in the middle of the table. Kian starts to relax with the heady aroma scent permeating the Lighthouse atmosphere. Hetta sets all the blessed cathedral candles in the correct places throughout the room. The atmosphere is serene, beautiful, and ready to begin the spiritual journey.

Kian, Toby, Oscar, and Hetta sit around the candlelit table. Hetta sits across from Kian. A large bowl of water and a large glass container is now in the middle of the table. Oscar takes a deep breath then instructs Kian. "Raise your arm and place your hand over the water." Kian pauses, seeking reassurance, and then regards Toby, who nods, encouraging Kian to follow Oscar's instruction. Hetta also nods her head to reassure Kian, as this metaphysical work is foreign to Kian. "This is to be a major lesson on your spiritual journey. That is why you must trust us." Oscar's eyes are shut tight. He remains calm but serious as he instructs Kian again, "Relax, breathe with us." Kian looks at Toby again. Toby nods. Kian becomes more comfortable with the process, then closes her eyes and starts to breathe in sync with Oscar, Hetta, and Toby, and then Kian extends her arm over the bowl of water.

Hetta gently clasps hold of Kian's arm and guides her hand over the water. A bluish light begins to glow around their hands. Hetta smiles squeezes Kian's hands tighter. The blue light seeps from Kian's hand and into the bowl of water. Kian opens her eyes and stares at the bowl in disbelief. The water has turned an iridescent blue.

The water in the bowl begins to swirl faster and faster. The mist rises and radiates out upwards and broader on the tabletop.

Kian's arm begins to shake from the surge of energy. Hetta stares into the swirling blue water. Suddenly Oscar stiffens and arches up in his chair. Hetta assertively speaks to the large swirling blue mist, "Show yourself." Hetta demands. Oscar smiles in anticipation and demands, "Tell us what you want."

A soft blue light begins to pulse from beneath Oscar's glasses. Oscar slowly raises his glasses and sits them on his forehead, revealing his blue eyes now glowing so brightly.

He speaks, not in his usual tone of voice, but in a weird feminine voice that speeds up and slows down as if it were a tape recording. Oscar is now in a trance. As the feminine voice emanates from Oscar's mouth, the ethereal resonance becomes more robust and more defined "... Kian ... Kian."

Kian's eyes fill with terror. She tries to pull away, but Hetta tightens the grip on Kian's hand. Hetta directs a question toward Oscar to the Spirit's voice, "What do you want?"

The water in the bowl swirls faster, glowing brighter and the color more brilliant. Oscar reaches out in a trance and gently touches Kian on the shoulder. "To finish what we started. To be free." Hetta whispers to Kian, "Don't be frightened. The longer a soul has wandered, the stranger their voice may seem." Hetta nods to Toby. Toby reaches down and lifts a container full of warm melted wax. He gets up and slowly pours the melted wax into the large glass container. Then Toby throws a towel over it and sits back down next to Kian.

Hetta takes charge, "I ask that you show yourself ... materialize your soul ... so that we may better understand your Spirit, your journey." She releases her grip on Kian. Suddenly the water stops twirling. The blue light dissipates from Oscar's eyes. He snaps out of his reverie, slumping back, exhausted. A powerful gust of wind rushes in, and candles blow out. Darkness, then the still of silence, remains. Kian sits rigid, a whiter shade of white. She whispers to the others, "What now?" Hetta remains respectful to the process

Quiet! Stillness prevails. The glowing water in the bowl spirals slowly out from the bowl then seeps straight through the towel and into the wax container.

The wax container starts to pulse a golden light, bathing

the room and their faces in a beautiful honey-colored hue. Then the container of wax starts to shake violently. The more it vibrates, the more its light intensifies, forcing everyone to shield their eyes from its intense beams.

Then the shaking instantly stops, and once again, the light disappears. Blackness. Stillness. Toby strikes a match and happily lights the candles. He regards Kian with his charismatic charm. Observing her deathly white face, "You O.K.?"

Kian can only nod. Toby turns to Hetta and the very drained Oscar. "What about you guys?" Hetta was accustomed to this whole metaphysical process and answered for both of them, "We're fine."

Hetta, excitedly curious, leans in towards the container of wax, observing it for a moment, still covered with the towel. Hetta turns to the rest of them. She gently grabs the towel covering the bowl, "Well then. I suppose we better have a peek at what our Ossian looks like. They all sit with anticipation as Hetta pulls away from the towel. She flings off the towel. Kian is stunned. So is Toby.

Hetta is so surprised. She gawks in disbelief, scrambling to come to terms with what lies before her.

In the overly large glass bowl, staring out at them all, from within the quick setting ghostly-white wax, is an impression of a newborn baby's face. In silence, they look at the wax impression. Kian felt confused, suffering in silence. She stepped back, wondering if this was a picture of her unborn baby that became a victim of her miscarriage. Kian puts a hand over her mouth, leaning in to define the vision in the wax.

Hetta observes Kian's grief and ever so compassionately places a loving arm around Kian's shoulder to help her digest the vision. Hetta gently asks, "Have you lost a child" Kian, devastated, nods her head, holding back the tears. Toby looks at Kian, surprised and empathetic. Toby attempts to support Kian through the moment, probing for more information for him to understand her buried pain,

"Was this recently?" Toby rubs Kian's back, trying to soothe her sadness. Due to his blindness, Oscar is unsure what is in the wax impression left by the ghost, which has so drastically changed the atmosphere. Hetta lovingly reassures Oscar by rubbing his arm. He settles quickly from her loving touch. Kian, overwhelmed, decides to usher Toby, Hetta, and Oscar to the front door.

They are all very reluctant to leave Kian in this state. As the tears still roll down her beautiful, emotionally wounded face, Toby asks, "Are you sure you'll be O.K.?' Kian bites her quivering lip, unable to express words. Kian nods her head repetitively and physically ushers them to the door. Kian finally musters up her voice, "Thanks, but I just need to be alone." Hetta offers to stay with Kian for support. Kian refuses help, reiterating that she will be O.K., explaining she needs time to digest the complexity of what just happened and what it all means.

Hetta says, "O.K. dear, but if you need anything, please don't hesitate to call. We are all here for you. When you start delving into the spiritual world, dear, it can be confronting. The only way out is through, and we are here to help you keep going through safely to the other side. Now things are much unexplained with the wax impression, and we can revisit this at the appropriate time to see what lies beneath the experience, to unravel the meaning, mystery, and the message from the ghost." Hetta reaches out and hugs the resolute emotional Kian, who nods gratefully back to Hetta. Kian, desolate, looks across to the unsure Toby. Hetta lovingly guides Oscar and Toby out the enormous old Lighthouse front door into the darkness of the billowing stormy night.

Kian closes the door tightly shut, leaning into it, before giving way to the flood of tears from the deep torrents of the emotional pain she has held in over the loss of her child.

Fifteen

Hours on, Kian now stands under the running shower, scrubbing herself aggressively. She suddenly stops, turning limp from the emotional fatigue. She slowly slides down to the bottom of the shower and continues to weep.

Later, as the hour ticks past, Kian has lost all sense of time. She sits down in front of the dressing table in her robe, looking at herself in the mirror and combing her beautiful long black wet hair. Realizing the life has drained from her face, she is a deathly color of gray. Kian sits down at the table with a bottle of red wine. She pours herself a glass of wine, her hands shaking. She gulps the wine, pours herself another drink, and gulps that down too.

Kian wanders in and grabs another bottle of wine. She notices the loose pages of her manuscript stacked next to Hetta's book on automata on the sideboard. She picks up the book, gazes at it, her mind racing. Suddenly she screams at the walls: "Why?" So frustrated, she hurls the book across the room. "It wasn't my fault! Grief-ridden, she slumps to her knees. "Why are you following me?"

Sudden silence reigns. Her vision shifts to the ceiling. Kian regains her composure. She glares at the manuscript. Then she gets to her feet, scoops up Hetta's book, and grabs the manuscript on the way out.

Kian, still carrying Hetta's book and the manuscript, heaves the front door open and steps out into the windy mist of the dark night. Kian stops by the cliff edge with a blank expression on her face. Thick fog obscures the ocean below. Kian tosses Hetta's book over the cliff. Then she pulls out the portable gas igniter from her pocket. She fires it up. Its flame illuminates her face as she slowly raises it towards her manuscript and sets the pages on fire.

Kian gazes at the pages burning in her hand for a moment. Then impulsively, she tosses them over the side of the cliff and watches their fiery descent beneath the blanket of fog in the dark of the night. The burning pages spiral and plummet down into the deep abyss of the raging ocean below. She watches them diving as they bounce off and shed firelight onto the monolithic black rocks that lead the way down into the perilous ocean waves.

Sixteen

Kian is fast asleep. Her face suddenly contorts with pain. We enter her nightmarish vision again.

On a wet, windy night, a long-haired woman lies dead with the Clan Clad Sword wedged in her stomach. We move closer. The face now looks faintly familiar. Closer still, it is Kian. A female voice whispers. "Kian, Kian."

Kian's eyes instantly fly open. She sits up rigid, realizing that she is in her bed and has had a bad dream, her face enmeshed with horror. She grabs the blankets and cowers against the bedhead. Realizing that a black shrouded shape is sitting at the foot of Kian's bed, visible now bathed in the moonlight. Frightened, Kian yells, "No, please no!"

Vulnerable, she crouches, frozen with fear as the black shrouded shape whispers in the same eerie voice from the séance. Ossian, now gentle but stern, "My favor must be repaid." The black shrouded shape gracefully stands slowly, her features slightly concealed beneath the sheer black-veiled hood.

Kian strangely recognizing Ossian, Kian's fear subtly subsides for a moment, and then curious Kian speaks, "Ossian?"

Ossian glides closer. Kian reels back, leaning heavily onto the bedhead. "No! Get away from me!" Suddenly Ossian reaches out and plunges her hand straight into Kian's abdomen. Stunned and breathless, Kian watches helplessly as Ossian feels within her womb. Ossian makes a very bold, clear, strong statement, "You are with child." Ossian swiftly removes her hand from Kian's abdomen. Kian was stunned by what had just happened. Ossian then states even more clearly in a matter-of-fact tone, "A daughter," Kian gasps to catch her breath. Shocked by Ossian's act, she then sits bolt upright. Ossian has now gone, dissolved into thin air.

Kian, stunned, grappling to make sense of it all, checks her stomach. Nothing, no sight of any incision or blood. She nauseously slumps back, dazed and confused. Kian searches herself again, studying her abdomen. No physical damage at all visible. Kian rechecks herself, wondering for a moment if she is in some sort of dream state before realizing she isn't.

Sitting on the bed, she contemplates Ossian's words. What was that about, she thinks over and over? Asking herself the question is this real and then, in her desperation, if this may be possible and could this be her dream come true. Her eyes soften to a starry-eyed look thinking of such a long-awaited wish and its possibilities.

Then she fobs of all those thoughts as being ridiculous. Convincing herself that Ossian is playing on her vulnerability as some sort of a game, and Ossian somehow knows her emotional wound and knows that all Kian so desperately wants is her own child. Kian eventually falls to sleep, but it is a very restless slumber of continued tossing, turning, and unable to enter the fifth realm of sleep to really settle. Kian's analytical mind continues to process Ossian's strange ghostly behavior and haunting words to make sense of Ossian's mephisto-phelian act. Kian decides she needs to make some serious decisions.

Seventeen

It is bleak, miserable, and pouring with rain, Kian's long black hair covered by a long hooded raincoat, further protected by a black umbrella. Kian steps out from the clinic door and trudges along the street, looking a little bewildered. She stops suddenly, staring at something across the road.

Toby and an attractive young woman, late 20's, kiss and cuddle under an umbrella outside Toby's shop. The woman kisses Toby passionately full on the mouth, climbs into an expensive sports car, and roars off as he watches her leave. Toby waves goodbye.

Kian instantly falls into a rage of jealousy, then emotionally backtracks. She retreats to hide, deciding irrationally to go into the nearest coffee shop to collect herself from what she has just observed. Kian can't settle her rage. She attempts to drink the warm brew and is overcome by a wave of anxious nausea. She stares heartbroken and lonely at the heavy waterfall of raindrops falling on the large glass windowpane as she continues looking out onto the street across to Toby's shop.

Impulsively she stands up from the chair with a look of

direct intent and angrily marches out into the rain and across the road into Toby's shop.

When Kian enters the empty shop, Toby quietly comes out from the backroom and pecks Kian's cheek. Cheekily he acknowledges her. "Hey, baby." Kian's face bore a look of great disdain. "Hi." Toby excited, not noticing her rage, "I got some great news! The publisher loved the sample chapters. They cannot wait for the rest of the manuscript. Kian responds with a snide serpent's tongue, "Good."

Toby joyously agog responds quickly back to Kian, validating the great opportunity with, "Good? It is better than good. We could be talking six-figure advance." He searches her face for some positive reaction. Kian angrily blurts out, "I'm pregnant." Toby stops dead in his tracks, absolutely dumbfounded, his eyes wide and completely stunned by what she has just said. "What?" His tone is of utter disbelief, unsure if he heard her right. Kian raging with anger, curtly states loudly, "I'm pregnant." Kian, so serious staunchly stands, regarding Toby's reaction. Quizzically he asks, "You sure?"

Kian assertively nods her head. Suddenly the doorbell rings as a couple of customers enter. Toby ushers Kian to the side of the counter, whispering and clinically states, "You can't be! It's gotta be your husband's!"

Kian looks at him in shocked disbelief, feeling the coldness of the rejection in his statement. Vehemently challenging him, she quips back, "Impossible."

Toby banters back, "Why?" Kian flying on the attack, "We separated and haven't been together for months." Toby grappled from the shock of the news, still questioning with veracity, "Are you sure? Are you sure it's mine?" Kian, hostile from his words, aggressively nods her head again.

Toby still denies any inclination that it may be his and any ownership of his part in this scenario.

"Shit! No way is this happening!" Kian, not expecting his reaction to this news to be so cold, uncaring, and so disowning, brutally retaliates, "Believe me, it is." The customers leave the shop. Toby, in a demanding tone, "What are you gonna do?"

Kian glares at him with the sad wave of rejection sweeping across her face, "What do you mean?" Toby dominating heartless, "you can't have it!" Kian glares at him, welling up with emotion, as he continues on, "It's just not right!" her eyes widen in anger, her lips pursed, "You don't understand. I have responsibilities, priorities." Kian sarcastically, "Yes, I know. I just saw you with her." When caught off guard, Toby savors the comment for a beat, then, "I tried to tell you." Kian, once again, back like an avalanche with her words, "You could have left." Toby frustrated, "You wouldn't let me." Kian backs up her statement, "After that first time, you could have gone and never come back." Toby shakes his head, frustrated with her childlike response, appeasing again to her intellect, "You didn't want to listen." Kian loses control yelling at him, "Why did you come back?!" Toby was momentarily distracted by the two customers standing peering in from outside the front window, then observing them move away.

Toby turns to confront Kian again. "Look, I am attracted to you. And I do have feelings for you. But you're still married, Kian. And now I'm going to marry someone else."

Kian stares at him, unable to move, unable to breathe.

Shot down by his words. Toby sighs ambiguously, stating, "I felt we both understood we were sharing a sensual energy, that's all." Overwhelmed and enraged by his arrogance and dismissal of her feelings, Kian furiously leaves the shop, slamming the door almost to a shattering point as she swiftly vacates the building.

Eighteen

Hetta sits warming herself by the fireplace, concentrating on something she's writing onto a pad. The doorbell chimes. Hetta puts down the writing pad, checks the time. It's midnight. The exquisite antique clock loudly rings out perfectly on time. The doorbell keeps chiming. Hetta frowns, gets up from her favorite antique armchair, and heads toward the front door. Hetta peers through the peephole and spies Kian, drenched, shivering profusely, standing on the front porch, her long black mane of hair soaked, and all her clothes soaked through from the rain. Kian appears emotionally drained.

Hetta, surprised, quickly grabs the large gold brass set of keys and, fumbling, unlocks the door. Hetta hurries, now so concerned for Kian's chaotic state. "Oh my goodness!"

She opens the door. Kian, sad and bedraggled, stands there shivering in the rain with tears rolling down her beautiful face. Her long black, saturated hair flaps in the stormy wind. Her voice quivers as she attempts to validate herself to Hetta,

"I ... just, I had to ... I had nowhere else to go." Hetta's concern ushers her inside the iconic estate home. Reassuring her, "Quickly dear, before you catch your death!"

Oscar appears, in his dressing-gown, holding on to the side rail of the wall for support and orientation. He politely inquires to the women, checking if everything is O.K. Kian responds shakily, "Oscar, Hi." Now aware that something is wrong, Oscar more assertively directs his line of question to the women one more time.

Hetta, in her sweet manner, reassures him, "Nothing to concern yourself with, dear. Just a little late-night woman's business, that's all. I am just going to help Kian get warm and dry and make her a cup of tea." Oscar sensing something seriously wrong, kindly offers to put the kettle on while the women have a chat.

Hetta takes Kian to the bathroom, where she can change into some of Hetta's dry clothes. Oscar stokes the fire up so it will be warm when they come back into the room. The two women move back into the large drawing-room. Hetta directs Kian to sit in a beautiful, comfortable chair close to the fire to warm herself up. As gentlemanly as ever, Oscar realizes it's time to make his exit. He bids Kian goodnight and then leaves. Kian, beginning to get warmer, bids Oscar a friendly goodnight.

Kian now sits by the fireplace, out of her wet clothes and wearing one of Hetta's expensive dressing gowns. Hetta approaches, handing Kian a glass of Brandy. Kian hesitates for a moment while Hetta reassures her in a motherly tone, "Go on. It'll warm you up." Kian adamantly declines the drink. Hetta adjusting her aristocratic grey bun on top of her head and, looking over her half-eye gold-rimmed glasses, says,

"Don't worry, and it won't hurt the baby. "Kian shoots her a surprised, shocked look. "He told you!"

Hetta nodding stops mid-conversation and chooses her words very carefully so as not to appear to have taken sides. Hetta sheds some light on the topic, which Kian seems to soften to on hearing, "He's beside himself. He doesn't know what to make of it." Hetta regards Kian as her tears well up as she sits in silence, pondering Hetta's' statement. Hetta sits quietly for a moment and sips her brandy.

Hetta breaks her silence and continues in a pleasant reverie, "Mind you, it comes as no surprise. What, with all the sparks and romantic dalliances between you two." Kian feels supported by Hetta and painfully explains that Toby is dead against her having the baby. Hetta says with inner knowing, "What you decide for you is what matters." Kian responds, "I want it. There's no way I can give this child up." Kian stares intensely into Hetta's eyes and starts to weep softly, repeat-ing that she will not get rid of the baby. Hetta picks up a hairbrush and gently brushes Kian's long straight black hair, which is now starting to dry by the firelight.

Hetta opens up, sharing a little more about herself, "I never had children. Not because I couldn't, but because I wouldn't. She lifts her sleeve, exposing the two scars on her wrist. "How can someone with such an unknowing disregard for their own lives and the gifts they have been given ever consider being responsible for someone else's?"

It took me years to understand that I was different and a seer. Many people of this caliber book themselves into psychiatric facilities thinking they're weird, not accepted, or have mental health issues. In fact, they're very clairvoyant and have not accepted this about themselves and just haven't found the right people to connect with to help them discover their gifts. Because of this scar, I learned about myself and my gifts. And it has been an extraordinary journey, and I have been able to help many people. If I had a child, I would not have been able to afford the time to be on my set path. I would never have been fortunate enough to meet my soul mate Oscar, who is such a blessing and provides such an abundance of love in my life."

Kian's attention has shifted from her grief to admiration for Hetta's words of wisdom and inspiration learned from her painful past. Kian respectfully acknowledges Hetta's story, "I guess life can be unforgiving." Hetta raises her glass to salute Kian, "As long as it's not unfulfilled."

Kian smiles back at Hetta, feeling far more hopeful than when she first arrived at the house. Kian wonders why all this is happening in her life right now.

Hetta soothed Kian further, "It's your journey in life, dear. Your path has brought you to this place and time for a reason. Perhaps to move forward...to be free of whatever plagues you." Kian shakes her head, disputing being so accessible. Hetta rushes in again with positive energy, "Of course you can. We all can. It's all just a matter of choice." Strangely Kian explains that she feels cursed. Hetta frowns for a second, not seeing this, continuing silently to sip more Brandy, then Kian begins to speak of her experience, softly and slowly, "I was living with my boyfriend. I was seventeen, and he was twenty. Anyhow, I got pregnant. He wanted nothing to do with it...or me if I had it. But I was young and in love and terrified of losing him, so I had the baby aborted. Sadly I deeply regretted it. It was a girl ."I quietly lived with the pain of that for a very long time.

Kian pauses, gazes into the fire, and then sighs. The bastard left me anyway. I never trusted any man again," Kian smiles for a moment reminiscent, "Not until Jason." Hetta regards Kian, very inquisitive she probes who Jason is and where he is now, "My husband. We both loved children so much. "We could never seem to have any." Hetta rubs Kian's shoulders, using a Reiki Energy Healing technique to help soothe Kian's past pain. As Kian continues, "For six years, we tried." She breaks down, feeling the emotional trauma of it all. "But I kept miscarrying ... three beautiful little souls ... all girls."

Hetta reassures Kian she is O.K. and that it is not her fault. However, Kian is still resistive to the joyous, supportive outpouring from Hetta. "I've been cursed... being punished for what I did to my first child!"

Hetta swiftly spins her around and looks her straight in the eyes, sternly stating, "That's nonsense. You hear me?" Kian quivered nervously, "No one knows what it's been like, especially the last one. Jason was there with me when the nurse brought the still-born child into us in a sports bag. She was five months formed, almost fully formed. I held her in my arms as if she were alive, but Jason, all he could see was her tiny, tiny, little blue face." Remembering the pain, she weeps, "He never got over it." Hetta hugs her, strokes her hair in a motherly fashion, feeling her pain. Kian then blurts out, "That's why I left Jason."

Hetta switches into trying to solve the ghost mystery and its significance to Kian's present situation, trying to marry up all the parties to help Kian find some resolve from her past pain and help her begin to move forward. "And Ossian? You think she's the soul of your first unborn?" Kian responds amidst her emotional turmoil, "I think she followed me here to the Lighthouse ... she used your book to get to me." Hetta looks on, considering the possibility and asking Kian why that would be. Hetta ponders on what Kian has just said and feels for a moment that this may well be a possibility. Kian continued, "She wants this baby! She wants to take it from me like she did the others!" Hetta frowns, disagreeing, and shakes her head. I don't know if I believe that entirely."

Kian pushed her theory further for recognition, "Neither did I. Not until I saw her face in the wax." Hetta reflective thinks about it. "You said it yourself. She had a plan, remember?" Hetta changes the topic inquiring if she has completed the manuscript.

Kian flips back on the defense. "I don't care about it. All I care about now is my baby." She takes a breath, realizing Hetta is not the enemy, "Yes, I have, and I gave it to Toby, who gave it to a publisher friend of his, supposedly." Hetta makes Kian another cup of tea, and they talk on into the night for a few more hours. Hetta suggests Kian stay with them for the night, as it is very stormy outside and dangerous to be driving at this time of the night in such a foreboding storm.

Nineteen

Kian pulls up in the Lighthouse driveway. It's almost sunset. Dark clouds in the distance herald a storm. An exhausted Kian gets out of the car. She looks out across the ocean at the approaching storm. Then she gazes up at the Lighthouse. Her mind contemplating what she must do. As the mild sunlight softens through the Lighthouse window and the dark arises again, Kian flings open the wardrobe door and rummages through her clothing, and tosses it into her suitcase on her bed. Kian throws food, cups, saucers, cutlery, and whatever else she can get her hands on into a large cardboard box. Kian heaves her bulging suitcase and the cardboard box into the boot of her car. Kian notices her porcelain fairy doll still propped up against the window on returning to the kitchen. She picks up the fairy doll, smiles at it, then rubs her stomach tenderly.

Kian lies submerged in a hot bath with half a consumed bottle of wine alongside her. The fairy doll sits on a chair next to her clothing. Humming and hawing, Kian picks up her cell phone. Flicks through the phone book contacts, then she stops at "JASON." She hesitates. She looks at the fairy doll. Then she presses the number. Kian listens as the phone rings. Jason answers urgently, "Kian? Where have you been? I've been worried sick about you!" She waits for a minute in silence. With apprehension, she begins to speak, "... Jason ... I'm ....." Jason grapples to understand what's going on." Kian breaks down, "I'm sorry. I just..."

Jason is overly zealous, "Where are you?" Kian doesn't answer and remains in deadly silence. "Please, honey, don't hang up." Another long pause, as Jason continues to persist on the phone. Kian then bluntly expresses her fear in very few words. Jason still persistent on the phone, "Tell me where you are. I'll come and get you." The cell phone suddenly flies from Kian's hand! It smashes onto the old slate-tiled floor. Then the lights in the bathroom begin to flicker madly. Kian sinks into the water. Then, by Kian's feet, at the other end of the bath, Ossian's shrouded head slowly emerges from the water.

We cannot distinguish any distinct features beneath the thinly veiled hood, just a nose and mouth. Ossian opens her mouth. Grey ectoplasm oozes out, which then envelopes Kian in a shadowy cocoon. Kian freezes, unable to do anything but watch the ghost's actions. Ossian raises her arms. More ectoplasm streams from her fingertips and gathers just above the water like a fog. Ossian gestures hypnotically. The mist swirls slowly, forming a turning three-dimensional image of a newborn baby girl. Ossian's chilling voice reigns out, and fear rises in Kian's heart, "Remember our pact." The image of the baby dissolves. Then Ossian slides back under the water and disappears.

Kian, overwhelmed, shaking profusely, clambers out of the bath, throwing on her robe. Kian attempts to run after

Ossian, aggressively shaking her hand to the air. "Stay away from my baby! Do you hear me?!" Ossian suddenly reappears, standing just behind Kian wearing a flowing robe. "We made a pact."

Kian, completely caught off guard, fires back, "Get out! Get out! Leave me alone" Ossian, strong with intent and vigilant, "We have little time. You Kian must repay my favor." Kian rebelled and screamed back, "No! I don't want to write anymore! Not like this!" The shutters in the Lighthouse begin to clatter violently. Ossian is adamant, "You will."

As Ossian slowly pulls back her thin veil hood to reveal a beautiful young woman with long dark curly hair and wild blue eyes, she leans closer to Kian; her tone softens, "You must."

Ossian disappears. The shutters slam tight with a thunderous bang. Breathless, Kian dashes out of the room. Kian scrambles toward the front door. A minute too late! The bolts slide shut! Kian fights as her waif-like body struggles to release them. No luck. Ossian suddenly appears behind her again, goading Kian, "We have work to do." Kian yells, refusing to be dominated. Ossian disappears again. Kian exasperated screams ferociously back at the walls.

Exhausted from the encounter, Kian slumps to her knees, flops to the floor, and leans into the wall. Silence. Ossian's voice emanates from within the confines of the Lighthouse walls, "No harm will come to the child. But you must do as we agreed and finish what has begun". Kian, exasperated, looks up into the air questioning the motive of the ghost, "If I do it. If I finish it, you will let me and my baby go?" Kian waits in the haunting silence and receives no response. Kian screams, beckoning a response from Ossian.

Ossian's tones shift, and for a moment, Kian is confused and emotionally steps back a level from the situation with her rage. Ossian softens and is almost vulnerable. She explains, "It is why I am here. It is my sad story, and you are the only source that can help me. And you promised you would tell my story. It is destined."

Kian, surprised, suddenly drops her fear and collects herself, pondering Ossian's words. Kian is now more in control of her emotions and reigning in fathoms of fear for the mystic, "Promise me you'll let us go!"

Ossian speaks softly again, "Finish the story properly the way I want the ending to occur. Finish it, and all will be released."

Kian abruptly sits in silence, the quiet hauntingly loud, as she begins to assess all the goings-on from the time she set foot in the Lighthouse and starts to see with hindsight how things have transpired. It would appear the reason why is now becoming a little clearer. Kian agonizes over her next move and wonders at what cost it will be to her. Given that she understands she had made a pact and that perhaps it may have worse repercussions if she breaks her promise. Kian decides to commit to freedom for both their souls.

Kian sits at the table, illuminated by a candle. Outside, the weather has gone wild, and wind, rain, thunder, and lightning now assault all her senses. Kian takes another swig of wine straight from the bottle. Kian calls out in a much kinder tone the air to Ossian. "Let's get on with it." She takes a deep breath. Her eyes glaze over, and the surge of adrenaline rushes through her veins. She starts to scribble onto the pad. As she sits there scribbling, we hear Kian's voice reciting the words she writes, as the story rolls onward, "And so it was to be the end they were destined for, but never deserved." Kian suddenly starts visualizing the event. It is so vivid that her attention is fixed on the scene and where it's taking her. Kian writes faster and faster, adding details as swiftly as possible. The vision has taken her to the coastal road, but back, far back in time, way back into the 17th century and well into the dark of the wet, gloomy foreshadowed night.

We see someone trudging awkwardly along the headland against the wind and rain. As Kian moves closer to observing the vision, she realizes it is A beautiful young woman, who is very heavily pregnant, her wild long black locks covering her frail-looking features.

Kian's voice portrays the story again as she writes the words, "She was weak of will and heavy with his child." Triggered by her own words, Kian starts to become short of breath as she still glares into the vision. The beautiful young woman arrives at the 17th century tavern. She peeps through the candlelit window into the crowded Tavern filled with men. It would appear she has caught someone's attention. She waves to him then steps back onto the cobbled path standing patiently under the glowing tall street lantern. A tall man in a black hooded cloak staggers out from the Tavern and into the rain.

Kian continues writing intensely and verbalizes the account, while at the same time observing the vision unraveling, "While he... he was heavy with ale... and fear... and hatred", The young beautiful pregnant woman sits calmly on the old low rock wall as the rain teems down. Suddenly she looks up unperturbed as the tall cloaked man emerges from the darkness. She smiles lovingly to acknowledge his presence. Kian still with the voice running in her head, "He had come to make good on his promise to take her and his child to a far-off life ... a better life." The beautiful young woman joyfully runs to him, embracing him as the rain streams down her beautiful face. "But his promise was as crooked as his soul." The tall cloaked man suddenly reaches beneath his cloak, swiftly as a warrior pulling out a Clan Clad sword. He grabs her throat aggressively. Unsuspecting of his intent and actions, the young pregnant woman suddenly realizes he is serious. She screams and fights to break free of his firm grip. But he ferociously knocks her to the ground, looming over her. His muscular arm raises the sword for the attack. The pregnant woman screams for mercy, her fragile hand reaching up defensively to protect her stomach and her unborn child. Still running the voice in her head, Kian recites, "Her screams became one with the wind... as the tall cloaked man slashes the sword down, straight into the pregnant woman's stomach, slicing into her. Again... and again... and again. Finally, he stops staggers back. The pregnant woman lies lifeless on the ground as the rain beats down on her lifeless face. He knows she is dead, sprawled at his feet with the sword wedged in her stomach, and then, all was quiet."

Lightning reveals the tall cloaked man, now frantically digging into the earth beside a massive, monolithic rock formation. Kian continues her voice sullen from the sadness "...and forgotten..." Kian gasps, free from her terrifying visual reverie. Experiencing an epiphany Kian holds her hand over her mouth, now understanding this was Ossian's cruel tragic death and her need to right the wrong. Kian sits tights on the chair rigid, then, breaking her silence, speaks out aloud to Ossian, this time for the first time with enormous compassion, "So Ossian, were you killed? Murdered! Is that what happened?" Deathly quiet reigns through the Lighthouse. Her words echo as she awaits Ossian's response for a moment, but still nothing. The front door unbolts, then slowly creaks open as the fog rolls in. Kian, surprised, observes what is happening. She slowly gets up from her chair, now sensing what she must do. Kian stops at the open front door of the Lighthouse, peering into the foggy night. Her eyes light up. A glowing orb has appeared and hovers like a beckoning beacon in the distance. Kian, mesmerized, follows and walks cautiously through the fog. She is following the Orb as it glides through the night, hovering over near the old cemetery on the Lighthouse grounds, positioning itself closer to the hundred-year-old bent strong tree swaying mercilessly in the wind.

Twenty

Hetta and Oscar are fast asleep, huddled lovingly together in the warm, safe confines of their elaborate estate home. Oscar appears to be in deep, peaceful slumber. Lying flat on his back Oscar takes a deep breath, and from his nose, blood starts to trickle, then slowly drip down onto his lips, then into his mouth. He suddenly bolts upright, his damaged eyes fully exposed. He gargles and then gasps for air. Hetta, a light sleeper, suddenly wakes up. Checking in on Oscar, asking him if he's O.K. Hetta aware Oscar is oblivious and in a trance-like state, Hetta is familiar with this happening to Oscar, and over the years, this has occurred to him quite often. Hetta, comfortably aware of this trance-like state, probes him gently, searching for an answer to what he is experiencing and channeling, "What is it? What do you see?" Oscar, now straight, upright in the bed, gasps, "The past! It is here! With us! With Kian!" Hetta asks what Kian has to do with this trance, what is happening, and what he sees. Oscar aloud prophetically states that Kian is in danger. Hetta, dumbfounded by his prophecy, notes that his nose bleeds and grabs a tissue to mop up the slight trickle of blood streaming down toward his mouth. Hetta goes through the motions to help Oscar come back to the earthly realms, realizing they must make haste and hurry to find Kian, for whatever foreboding situation is about to unfold. They quickly dress and vacate their home, out into the dark of the stormy night.

The Orb flies over the cliff, then downward rapidly descending deep down below then hovering, stopping mid-air at the jagged foot of the rocks beneath. Kian steps up, swiftly following the journey in hot pursuit, gazing at the Orb down below as she searches her immediate surroundings. The Orb hovers toward a spot as the light in the bleak, dark landscape intensifies, casting light across the atmosphere then transforming into the physical presence of Ossian. Kian watches as Ossian slowly spins in mid-air, more in wonder than fear. Then disappears, plummeting rapidly straight down the cliff's edge below and into the earth below. Kian holds tight on the spot where she stands.

A while later, and it's drizzling again. With adrenaline rushing through Kian's veins, Kian makes haste and races to her car to keep trailing Ossian. The headlights of Kian's car light up the road, following down along the area around the rock formation. She arrives safely in her car at a clearing way below where the Lighthouse stands atop of the monolithic rocks.

Kian races over to the muddy ground, where she now sees Ossian dissolve down. Kian swiftly grabs the shovel from her car boot. She digs frantically in the spot where Ossian may have vanished in the 17th century. She digs like a maniac, trying to find evidence to appease her mind and find answers. She hits something with her shovel. Getting down on her knees, suddenly realizing she has dug around four-foot square into the muddy ground, then carefully with both hands, uncovering what looks to be ancient old rags. Then she keeps on digging. Moments pass as Kian stands up. She wipes the rain and sweat from her brow after her feverish dig. Then she looks down with a ghoulish expression at her discovery. At her feet lies what appears to be a body tied up in old rags. Kian, feeling apprehensive, studies this for a moment. Hesitant, she then reaches down very cautiously and slowly to untie the rotting rope. She pulls a rubber glove out of her pocket and puts it on as she touches the rope. With her rubber-gloved hand, she handles the rope. The body suddenly sits bolt upright, then snaps the frayed rope and throws off the shroud to reveal Ossian manipulating the skeletal remains! Kian, instantly scared, irrationally jumps back.

Ossian hovers above the grave's edge, sadly, silently gazing down the ancient remains. Kian moves closer to her. "I'm sorry. I was wrong. What you were trying to tell me, I got it all wrong?" Ossian's beautiful face, now much defined and visible, lit by the full moonshine, she respectfully smiles gently, "It is not over. Not for us." Ossian gestures with her hand, pointing over Kian's shoulder.

Her attention snaps urgently to behind where Kian stands. "Not yet." Stunned by her words, Kian spins quickly around to see a silhouette standing in front of the car's headlights. She shields her eyes from the bright beams of light. As a full battle shape rapidly strides toward her, a deathly chill resonates throughout her body. As he closes in on her, Kian is suddenly astonished to find it's Toby. He calls her name abruptly. Toby steps up closer to Kian and stands on the opposite side of the grave. He looks down at the muddy open, desecrated grave. The dark side of Toby's character emerges as he speaks aggressively, "What the hell's going on?" He steps down into the muddy grave and inspects the decomposed remains.

Toby stares at Kian, "What is this?" He picks up some of the old decomposed material he stares at it closely. Under the moonlight's rays, Toby appears somehow very different than when Kian has viewed him in the past. Uncomfortable, she remains silent to control the moment and keep herself safe. In a solid masculine tone, he demands, "How did you find it?" Kian still won't answer. Toby spots the Ancient Clan Clad Sword, half-buried in the muddy earth alongside the remains.

With adeptness, he reaches down into the shallows of the muddy grave, Skillfully he grasps the Sword hilt with both hands and slowly raises the rusty, mud-caked Sword from its ancestral burial place. Because of such a discovery over the course of moments, Toby convinces Kian to go back to the Lighthouse with him so they can view this fantastic historical piece in clear light and discuss its origin and decide what to do. What can they do with this treasure find? Kian stands fixed, empty emotionally by his comments, as the rain still comes down on them both and fills the desecrated grave covering the old decomposed muslin body bag. Deep in thought, she concentrates intensely, consciously aware of his material-istic motive regarding the historical extraordinary Sword.

Twenty-One

They have both returned now to the warm confines of the Lighthouse and changed into dry clothes. Kian is still a little on edge. Toby works away without the slightest notion of Kian's cautiousness. Full of enthusiasm for material gain, he has now cleaned the Sword and waves it around as he admires its ancient craftsmanship with great intrigue. Cheekily he asks her, "How much do you think it's worth?" His eyes intensely scan the sharp blade. Kian ignores the question, slightly subtly moving further apart from him, as Toby looks around, checking out the Lighthouse surrounds of where they are currently standing. "Got anything more to drink?" Kian quips, "It looks like you have already had enough to drink." He retorts back, rebellious and sarcastic, "Well, you know how it is. It ain't every day someone gets told they're going to be a first-time dad." Kian's heart quivers for a moment, and panic rises in her chest. Kian, defensive, questions him as to what he wants. Demanding, he comes back at her, cutthroat like a bolt of lightning, "I told you, a drink" He wipes his pursed dry lips and appears to be breaking into an angry sweat. Kian notices the unusual behavior he seems to be displaying for the first time. Kian tries to cut him off and tells him to leave as she is not in the mood for his lousy attitude. He retaliates her rejection with ferocity, "What the hell is your problem?" Kian musters up the strength and tries to physically usher him toward the front door, once again directing him to leave. Toby verbally fights her refusing to budge. She feels his wrath as he angrily spits out, "You come here from who the hell knows where, get me entangled in this mess of yours, then you tell me to leave? Who the hell do you think you are?"

Kian, slightly guilty, reweighs her words to calm him, "I think it's best if we talked about this when you're not so ...like a possessed demon. He slams the butt of the Sword down on the large kitchen table.

Toby's maddened voice sounds like a different person as he screams at her, "No! Fuck you!" Kian is unsure what is happening now as a raging wind has entered the kitchen, where they both stand a distance from each other.

Deathly silence immediately reigns between them both. Kian's waif-like body stands steadfast. She begins to feel drained and sighs from the overwhelming velocity of tension in the room, "What do you want?" Toby appeared possessed now paces like a warrior around the kitchen, slowly waving the Sword about with great strength and manual dexterity. Kian's fearfulness rises as his misogynistic words cut deep into her soul as he lashes out, "I know what I don't want." A long, tense beat passes between the two. Kian notices his rigid stance as he stands tall, momentarily overpowering her. Subtly she draws back to maintain her balance as he leers at her again with menace. "I don't want you to have this baby." Kian's eyes well with tears, her lip quivers, as she remains protective and loyal to her unborn child, as she reels from his wrath attempting to appease to his veracious side, gently she speaks, "I can't promise that."

Once again, Toby flies into a rage at her stubbornness. "Yes, you can. It's easy. You just go to your doctor, and you know." He swishes the Sword around threateningly, then callously, "A little nip, a little tuck ... and it's all gone and forgotten! No interruption to anyone's life." Her intuition pushing her to flee, she starts to back away from him. Moving toward the front door of the Lighthouse, slyly, unnoticed, she grabs her car keys. She bumbles her words nervously, "You think I did this on purpose? You think I wanted this?" As she keeps backing up towards the front door.

Toby scathingly slides closer, his eyes wild and have changed color. "Who the fuck knows what you were thinking? Kian realizes she is in serious trouble. She starts to shake, then begs, "Please, Toby, let's not do this." Toby lunges at her, seething, "That child will destroy my life!" Kian attempts to win him over, trying a getting-out scenario. "You don't have to be involved. It can be our secret." He screams at her, intolerant of her offer. "It'll look like me!" He hatefully glares straight at her. "Are you going to get rid of it?" Kian is now nearer the front door. Toby screams. It is so deafening the walls reverberate and echo with powerful devilish anguish, "Answer me! Answer me! He begins to come at her, yielding the Ancient Sword. Suddenly his arm goes weak, and it slips from his grasp. Quickly Kian turns to open the front door of the Lighthouse. She is so nervous she has trouble trying to open the lock. Toby focuses on the Sword on the floor in a trance-like state, his arm so heavy and weak. He tries to shake out the numbness, his voluminous anger rising again.

He suddenly lunges at her with the Sword, narrowly missing her. "Answer me!"

Kian, just at the exact moment, finally hauls the door open, dashing panic-stricken out the front door into the dark of the haunting night. Kian races into the thick fog. Lightning flashes, thunder rumbles in the distance. Toby chases after her, staggering and wildly wielding the hefty Ancient Sword.

Frantic and without thought, with nowhere else to go, Kian irrationally jumps into her car, locking all the doors, sliding down in the back seat attempting to hide in the darkness. Toby cased the area pacing around in the dark, trying to find where she may be hiding. Toby walks on further past the car. He heads back to the lighthouse front porch, then he suddenly stops by the car, observing the fog on the inside of the car window. Toby scans the darkness experiencing pain in his chest. Toby hits his chest and tries to catch his breath. His tone changes back to a familiar resonance. But still, Kian cannot trust as he calls out in the dark of the night, "It's okay! I won't hurt you!" Kian lies perfectly still, listening as Toby keeps yelling, trying to coerce her out of hiding. "I just wanna talk!"

Kian is thinking about reneging and debating whether she should oblige now he seems to have calmed down. She bites her lip holding her breath as Toby tests the front car door lock. Toby slowly strategically paces around the car, trying all the doors. He stops by the rear door. "We need to resolve this!" Then, in an almighty aggressive action, he smashes the

Sword through the back door window, spraying glass every-where. Kian screams. Toby sharply reaches in and opens the door, then grabs Kian by the hair in caveman-like action, attempting to drag her out. She fights back but is weak com-pared to his brute strength. Toby sadistically overpowers her and wrenches Kian out of the car, "No! Please! No!" Toby's eyes are wild with fury eyes as he drags her away, carrying her kicking and screaming down the gloomy rocks.

Toby recklessly flings Kian onto the ground alongside the open grave. He plants his boot on her chest, rendering her breathless and gasping, "No Toby, please! Stop!" Toby raises the Clan Clad Ancient Sword high above his shoulders. Kian raises her arm defensively to protect her stomach. She looks up into Toby's rage and is momentarily transported back into the vision in her written words of the story she channeled. The tall cloaked man looms over the very pregnant vulner-able, defenseless woman with his Clan Clad Sword. A flash of lightning reveals his face. Kian now sees back in time that the man in the vision is, in fact, Toby, as he savagely thrusts the Sword down into the vulnerable pregnant woman, who lay semi-conscious on the muddy ground, her head bleeding slumped against the rock wall.

Kian switches back into this lifetime as Toby accurately yields the Clan Clad Ancient Sword in her direction. Kian lets out a guttural scream, resisting. "No, Toby, no!" She fights to break free of his grasp, avoiding the total velocity of his brutal plunge at her with the dangerous weapon as she accidentally rolls into the marshy desecrated grave, painfully landing on top of the ancient skeletal remains. She grimaces in pain as her shoulder bleeds profusely lacerated by the acute sharpness of the Sword. Toby follows swiftly, stepping into the icy grave demonically looming over her. Snarling, he raises the Sword once again. Kian, dispirited, closes her eyes, breathless, whispering in desperation, "Ossian."

Toby is hurled backward, stunned, and rendered motionless with the wind knocked out of him with an explosion of blinding light. The mighty strong Sword flies savagely from his hand. And wedges itself tightly, handle first, between folds in the rocks. Ossian suddenly materializes into the physical form. She raises her strong hand. Toby attempts to rise, flabbergasted, he staggers back in horror.

Ossian lurches toward him. Toby reels back, losing his balance, slipping on the mud. He falls back straight onto the Sword, severing his jugular. Hetta arrives just in time to rescue Kian. Hetta is aided by the Police who observe everything. Toby drops down in front of the vulnerable Kian, blood spurting from his neck and pulsing outwards into the fog. In the bright light that now falls over them, their eyes lock for the last time. Abruptly his eyes dissolve back to his standard color. With his last breath, he manages a faint smile as the life force drains out of him, shakily his voice stammers, "S..o..rry." His ethereal soul instantly rises out of his body, turning the darkest shade of black, barbarically plunging downward, penetrating the mushy ground where he lays dead.

Kian, emotionally distraught, struggles to her feet as the shock sets in. The Police watch on in disbelief at the scene before them, having observed the chain of events, as Kian drags herself out of the algal wet marshy grave. As she stands there, staring down at Toby, who takes his final breath, now passing from this lifetime. Kian's eyes swell with tears of sorrow at the sudden loss and death of a soul whom she had feelings for, and she had shared such unforgettable experiences. She looks on heartbroken.

A hand reaches out from the fog and grabs her! Kian spins around, startled. Hetta steps forward out from the mist, which has now begun to lift. Hetta's gaze shifts as she spies Toby dead in the grave. Dismayed and aghast, she says, "My God! It's happened!" Kian acknowledges Hetta and her words. Hetta justifies her words to Kian, "Oscar had a strong vision, we knew you were in trouble, we got here as quickly as we could to warn you.

Hetta fleetly scrambles down to where Toby lay, "It was so strong! I had to come!" Hetta softly strokes Toby's blood-stained hair. "My God, no, no." I Love you like a son. I love you so.

Toby's body gargles as his lungs slowly drown in his blood. Kian, totally exhausted and bewildered by the whole psychic trauma, slumps down alongside the grave as she looks on as Hetta comforts Toby, even though he is dead. Hetta speaks to the air, to Toby's soul, "Can you hear me?" Toby, now deathly cold, just stares up with a vacant expression. Hetta leans closer into him.

"Don't be afraid. All of this .... Kian... the Lighthouse... Ossian ... me ... the baby... and what happened to you ... it all makes sense ... it was all meant to be in a metaphysical sense ... and so sad to happen like this. As we all know, one cannot change the course of our destiny no matter what, if some-thing is meant to be." Hetta gently squeezes Toby's hand. Her eyes tear up.

Ossian glides protectively over to Kian, her feminine voice

shedding her take on the traumatic situation just experienced by all. "All of us were needed to be here...to break the pattern...the karmic past, so we all can move forward in this lifetime."

Hetta reaches toward Toby. "I know you are sorry we are all here. Thank you, and may your spirit forgive you as you journey back safely into the light."

Kian forlorn turns to Ossian, "I'm sorry, Ossian. I'm sorry for what happened to you and your child." Hetta sweeps into the conversation shedding more light, "she didn't lose a child on that wretched night of long ago.' Kian looks at Hetta quizzically. "It was you, dear... you lost the child." Kian stares dumb, stricken as Hetta continues, "in your past life... you were the mother."

Kian spins around to Ossian, "And Ossian?" Ossian stands calm, explaining, "I lost my mother." Kian slumps back, stunned by the revelation, thinking back over the experiences of the past months taking in Ossian's words. "For three hundred years, I have been here waiting with her, Unblessed, unforgiven, and unknown."

Deep in thought over the words spoken, Kian protects her stomach, asking. "What about my baby? The ghost of Ossian gently touches Kian on the stomach and smiles. "She is perfectly safe. Her purpose is strong, her destiny written." Kian protective seeks clarity, "Purpose?' Now the ghost of Ossian is in a world of her own, "To help me fulfill my soul's journey, to be the great writer I am destined to be." Thunder rumbles and lightning flashes, "But first, I must have consent." Kian, slightly defensive, responds, "Consent?"

Hetta pipes up, understanding what is going on here,

with the metaphysical, "From you, Kian, to become one with your child." Kian's face turns to a dark frown as she regards Hetta, open-mouthed then up at Ossian. Hetta nods to Kian, "it's safe. No harm will come to your child. The spirit world will protect her." Kian, thinking deeply, starts to settle, now trusting Hetta's words. She takes a deep breath and nods her head to agree to this.

The ghost of Ossian beams light over all of them, "And so it is, and so it will be." Now given her freedom, Ossian dissolves into the light fog. Kian turns and looks back at Toby. A tear streams from her eyes. Kian notices that Toby, surrounded by Police attending to his dead body, now strangely appears peaceful. Under the Police's guidance, Hetta escorts Kian away from the scene.

Twenty-Two

"EIGHT YEARS LATER"

K ian dozes in her deckchair atop the monolithic cliffs. Her cell phone rings. She awakes and checks the caller ID, "JASON." She answers with a smile. "Is this my husband or my agent? Jason cheerfully responds, stating, "Both," he continues, "Early sales indicate another bestseller. Congratulations, honey, it looks like you'll be able to buy yourself another Lighthouse or two." Kian smiles, "Hurry home. We miss you."

Time marches on, and Kian is by the rock formation with a fresh-cut bunch of flowers in her hand. She stops to look down at Ossian and Toby's gravesites facing the vast ocean, encircled with white picket fences and white, wooden, unadorned crosses. Kian places the flowers gently at the foot of the graves. She looks up, distracted by a car horn that beeps in the distance. She turns to see. It's Hetta and Oscar. Hetta happily waves over to her, and Kian returns the wave, then cheerily heads toward them, then ushering them through the front door of the Lighthouse. Kian stops abruptly by the door. She opens it, entering slowly into the large room. A solid feminine influence now prevails with antique furniture, soft furnishings. Kian looks over to her fairy doll alongside other beautiful porcelain dolls with a fairy tale theme. A beautiful eight-year-old girl with curly long red hair and wild blue eyes sits cross-legged on the floor, surrounded by pages of a written manuscript.

She scrawls frantically onto a writing pad. She rips off a page, tosses it over her shoulder, and starts scribbling on yet another page. Kian watches her for a moment, relating to her own writing experience, then whispers lovingly, "Ossian?" The beautiful child looks up. "Daddy will be home soon."

The child gives her a warm, contented smile, "Do you mean Daddy number one or Daddy number two". Then the child returns to her work. Hetta, Oscar, and Kian smile at her words and leave her there, happy and fulfilled. Kian stops by another door. She opens it, steps inside. Kian, Hetta, and Oscar enter the room, the Lighthouse Light now fully restored to its former glory with the sparkling new Lens. Like the beautiful sunsets, a picturesque scene across the wild landscape Kian steps out onto the balcony and gazes out at dusk. She looks down at Ossian and Toby's gravesite. A smile forms across her contented face. Suddenly a hand pulls a lever, flicks a switch. A powerful ray of light suddenly explodes from the Lighthouse.

It sweeps out across the village, the headlands, the ocean, and finally, across Ossian and Toby's graves. Pulsing once ... then four times ... then three times. Kian, Hetta, and Oscar stand on the balcony, happily in the breathtaking moment, all united, holding hands, and we leave them there.

About the author

Karen Power has a unique and fresh approach to storytelling. Her writing draws on the essence of her life experiences and inherent natural affinity with the metaphysical.

She has worked as a nurse, screenplay writer, background extra, and has written several novels and screenplays. Karen is the producer, writer and director of a short film titled "Raphael", showcasing on Prime Video Amazon, which has won several International Awards.

Karen is the author of *The Lighthouse*, a supernatural romance thriller; *The Golden Phoenix*, a supernatural crime romance thriller; and *KAJO*, an Australian adventure romance. Her work is available in paperback, e-book and audiobook formats from your favourite bookstores. You can order online, or enquire with your local bookshop or library.

For more information about Karen's current and future works, please visit: **www.karenpowerfilms.com.au**

Thank you for supporting an Australian writer of original, creative content. If you have enjoyed this book, please consider writing an online review.

www.ingramcontent.com/pod-product-compliance
Lightning Source LLC
Chambersburg PA
CBHW070627120726
47909CB00004B/1357